Bhagavad Gita for Everyday Living

Swami Mukundananda is a world-renowned spiritual teacher, an international authority on mind management, and a bestselling author who earned his degrees from the prestigious IIT Delhi and IIM Calcutta. He worked with a multinational firm for a short while before renouncing a promising career to enter monkhood. He studied the Vedic scriptures at the feet of Jagadguru Kripaluji Maharaj. For four decades now, he has been sharing his vast knowledge through his books, lectures, and life-transformation programs.

Every day, Swamiji meets hundreds, and even thousands, of people from all walks of life. His steadfast positivity exudes hope, clarity, and a sense of purpose to those who connect with him. He has deeply influenced the lives of millions who have been drawn by his profound integrity, charismatic personality, and passion to serve. Despite his hectic schedule, those who encounter him experience his warmth and compassion, and feel deeply touched by his humility. Swamiji's lectures are humorous, his arguments are logical and well laid-out, and most of all, his advice is practical. His lectures on social media platforms are loved and followed by millions. Swamiji divides his time between India and the US.

swamimukundananda.org
facebook.com/Swami.Mukundananda
instagram.com/Swami_Mukundananda
linkedin.com/in/swamimukundananda
x.com/Sw_Mukundananda
youtube.com/c/swamimukundananda

Other Books by the Author

7 Divine Laws to Awaken Your Best Self
(Also available in Hindi)

7 Mindsets for Success, Happiness and Fulfilment
(Also available in Hindi, Gujarati, Marathi, Oriya & Telugu)

Bhagavad Gita: The Song of God

Golden Rules for Living Your Best Life

Ishavasya Upanishad

Nourish Your Soul: Inspirations from and Lives of Great Saints

Questions You Always Wanted to Ask
(Also available in Marathi)

Science of Healthy Diet

Spiritual Dialectics

Spiritual Secrets from Hinduism: Essence of the Vedic Scriptures

The Art & Science of Happiness

The Power of Thoughts

The Science of Mind Management
(Also available in Gujarati & Telugu)

Yoga for the Body, Mind & Soul

Books for Children

Essence of Hinduism

Festivals of India

Healthy Body Healthy Mind: Yoga for Children

Inspiring Stories for Children (set of 4 books)

Mahabharat: The Story of Virtue and Dharma

My Best Friend Krishna

My Wisdom Book: Everyday Shlokas, Mantras, Bhajans & More

Ramayan: The Immortal Story of Duty and Devotion

Saints of India

Bhagavad Gita
for Everyday Living

SELECTED VERSES
WITH KEY TAKEAWAYS

Swami Mukundananda

RUPA

First published by
Rupa Publications India Pvt. Ltd 2025
161-B/4, Gulmohar House, Yusuf Sarai Community Centre,
New Delhi 110049

Sales Centres
Bengaluru Chennai
Hyderabad Kolkata Mumbai

P-ISBN: 978-93-7003-522-5
E-ISBN: 978-93-7003-058-9

First impression 2025

10 9 8 7 6 5 4 3 2 1

Contents

Introduction 1

Chapter 1: ***Arjun Vishad Yog***
Lamenting the Consequences of War 7

Chapter 2: ***Sankhya Yog***
The Yog of Analytical Knowledge 13

Chapter 3: ***Karm Yog***
The Yog of Action 31

Chapter 4: ***Jnana Karm Sanyas Yog***
The Yog of Knowledge and the Disciplines of Action 41

Chapter 5: ***Karm Sanyas Yog***
The Yog of Renunciation 54

Chapter 6: ***Dhyan Yog***
The Yog of Meditation 61

Chapter 7: ***Jnana Vijnana Yog***
Yog through the Realisation of Divine Knowledge 78

Chapter 8: ***Akshar Brahma Yog***
The Yog of the Eternal God 90

Chapter 9: ***Raja Vidya Yog***
Yog through the King of Sciences 94

Chapter 10: ***Vibhuti Yog***
Yog through Appreciating the Infinite Opulences of God 105

Chapter 11: ***Vishwaroop Darshan Yog***
Yog through Beholding the Cosmic Form of God 113

Chapter 12: ***Bhakti Yog***
The Yog of Devotion 119

Chapter 13: ***Kshetra Kshetrajna Vibhag Yog***
Yog through Distinguishing the Field and
the Knower of the Field 129

Chapter 14: ***Guna Traya Vibhag Yog***
Yog through Understanding the
Three Modes of Material Nature 139

Chapter 15: ***Purushottam Yog***
The Yog of the Supreme Divine Personality 150

Chapter 16: ***Daivasura Sampad Vibhag Yog***
Yog through Discerning the Divine and Demoniac Natures 159

Chapter 17: ***Shraddha Traya Vibhag Yog***
Yog through Discerning the Three Divisions of Faith 164

Chapter 18: ***Moksha Sanyas Yog***
Yog through the Perfection of Renunciation and Surrender 170

Let's Connect 194

Introduction

There are two ways to acquire knowledge: the ascending process and the descending process. In the ascending process, we utilize our senses, mind, and intellect to learn about the nature of the Truth. Since they are made from the material energy, maya, they are imperfect and limited. As a result, we can never be completely sure about the accuracy and reliability of the knowledge acquired through them.

The descending process, on the other hand, is completely free from defects. When we receive knowledge from a perfect source, we can be assured it is flawless. For example, if we wish to know who our father is, we simply ask our mother as she is the authority on this topic. Similarly, in spiritual matters too, the descending process immediately gives us access to vast reservoirs of knowledge which would have taken ages of self-effort to unveil. The only criterion here is that the source from which we receive the knowledge must be infallible and trustworthy. The Vedas are a source of such descending knowledge.

Essence of the Vedas

The Bhagavad Gita is a comprehensive and easy-to-understand summary of the Vedas. *Bhagavad* means 'of God', and *Gita* means 'song'. Hence, the *Bhagavad Gita* literally means 'Song of God'. It is a dialogue that took place between the Supreme Lord Shree Krishna and His devotee Arjun, on the verge of the Mahabharat war.

The Bhagavad Gita is set in the sixth section of the Mahabharat called the Bheeshma Parva. It covers 18 chapters—from chapter 25 to chapter 42.

Since it encapsulates most of the important aspects of the Vedas, it is also called *Gitopanishad* or the *Gita Upanishad*. The Bhagavad Gita serves two important purposes as discussed below.

It Imparts Brahma Vidya

The quest to understand all of creation is a never-ending endeavour. There is a growing realization that the more we discover and learn, the more there is to be known. This makes one wonder if there is any one piece of knowledge which could explain everything that exists. According to the Vedas, there is such a science, called *Brahma Vidya*, or the science of the Absolute Truth.

The purpose of the Bhagavad Gita, above all else, is to impart Brahma Vidya. Knowledge that helps a person resolve immediate problems is one kind of enlightenment, while wisdom that dispels the root of ignorance to solve all problems in one shot is another kind of enlightenment. The Bhagavad Gita aims at this second kind of knowledge by destroying the darkness that has enveloped the soul since endless lifetimes.

Unable to deal with the emotional turmoil of warring with his relatives, Arjun turned to Shree Krishna. Shree Krishna did not just advise him on his immediate problem but went above and beyond to give Arjun a profound discourse on the philosophy of life.

It Teaches the Practice of Yog

For any science to be useful, it must address two aspects—theory and practice. Even the best theoretical knowledge is insufficient in itself to solve the problems of life. And if theory is not put into practice, it only serves the purpose of intellectual entertainment.

The Bhagavad Gita is not content with providing a lofty philosophical understanding; it also describes clear-cut techniques to implement its spiritual precepts in everyday life. These techniques of applying the science of spirituality in our life are termed 'Yog'. Hence, the Bhagavad Gita is also called *Yog Shastra,* meaning 'the scripture that teaches the practice of Yog'.

The Setting of the Bhagavad Gita

Though the Absolute Truth is eternally One, in different ages it expresses itself in varied locales that impart their unique flavour to its presentation. The teaching of the Bhagavad Gita, therefore, is not merely a generalized philosophy. It is the practical application of ethics to human life in a specific situation that serves as its setting. Since the message was exceedingly profound, the Bhagavad Gita required an equally problematic and insurmountable crisis as its background.

Arjun was a victim of a moral paradox. On the one hand, he was facing people who deserved his respect and veneration, such as his grandfather, Bheeshma, and his teacher, Dronacharya, among other elders. On the other hand, his duty as a warrior was to fight the war of righteousness. It seemed like a dilemma without any solution because even the fruits of victory could not justify such a heinous act. Bewildered, demoralized, and dejected with the events, Arjun surrendered to the Supreme Lord and supplicated Him for guidance on the proper course of action. It was in this state of Arjun's moral confusion that Shree Krishna set out to enlighten him.

Its Teachings Are above Cult and Creed

There is one kind of teaching that propagates a dogma, cult, or creed. There is another kind of teaching that propagates ideals and life principles that are supremely above all cults and dogmas. Scholars who regard the Gita as the fruit of some particular religious system do injustice to the universality of its message. The ideas it presents are not the speculations of a philosophic intellect; rather, they are the enduring truths of spiritual realities that are verifiable in our own existence and sojourn through life.

The Gita seeks the ultimate Truth for the highest practical utility, not for intellectual or even spiritual satisfaction, but as the truth that opens for us the passage from our present mortal imperfection to an immortal perfection. Consequently, we must approach it with a humble attitude full of faith to receive its message that can lead us to spiritual perfection.

Manual for Everyday Living

In these times, when all yearn for peace but perceive conflict everywhere, the Bhagavad Gita is an apt source of inspiration. After all, this was also the setting for the conversation between God Almighty and one of His devotees.

Under ideal circumstances, we could spend enough time on each verse of this beautiful scripture to truly understand its meaning. However, our ever-rushed and busy schedules do not permit us such a luxury. Keeping this in mind, *Bhagavad Gita for Everyday Living* distils wisdom from the original scripture for quick access and ready use. Key verses have been included along with brief commentaries, abridged from *Bhagavad Gita—The Song of God*. Thus, this powerpacked edition bestows readers with a pithy collection of the Gita's most profound wisdom, inspiring messages, and calls to action. It is a ready-to-use reference guide that enables us to imbibe the teachings of the Bhagavad Gita quickly and easily.

Chapter 1

Arjun Vishad Yog

Lamenting the Consequences of War

धृतराष्ट्र उवाच ।
धर्मक्षेत्रे कुरुक्षेत्रे समवेता युयुत्सवः ।
मामकाः पाण्डवाश्चैव किमकुर्वत सञ्जय ॥ 1 ॥

dhṛitarāṣhtra uvācha
dharma-kṣhetre kuru-kṣhetre samavetā yuyutsavaḥ
māmakāḥ pāṇḍavāshchaiva kimakurvata sañjaya

Dhritarashtra said: O Sanjay, after gathering on the holy field of Kurukshetra and desiring to fight, what did my sons and the sons of Pandu do?

King Dhritarashtra, apart from being blind from birth, was also bereft of spiritual wisdom. Attachment to his sons made him deviate from the path of virtue and usurp the rightful kingdom of the Pandavas. He was conscious of the injustice he had meted out to his nephews, and as a result, his guilty conscience pricked him about the outcome of the battle. So now, he inquired from Sanjay about the events on the battlefield of Kurukshetra, where the war was to be fought.

He asks Sanjay, 'Having gathered on the battlefield, what did my sons and the sons of Pandu do?' It is obvious that they had assembled together for the sole purpose of the war. So, it was natural that they would fight. Why did Dhritarashtra feel the need to ask what they did?

His doubt can be discerned from the words he uses—*dharma kṣhetre*, meaning the land of dharma (virtuous conduct). Kurukshetra was a sacred land. In the *Shatapath Brahman* of the *Yajur Veda*, it is described as: *kurukṣhetram deva yajanam* 'Kurukshetra is the sacrificial arena of the celestial gods.' It was thus the land that nourished dharma. Dhritarashtra was concerned that the influence of the holy land of Kurukshetra would arouse the faculty of *vivek* (discernment) in his sons, and they would regard the massacre of their cousins as reprehensible. Such thoughts would induce them to negotiate a peaceful settlement. Dhritarashtra felt great dissatisfaction at this possibility. He thought if his sons agreed to a truce, the Pandavas would continue to remain an impediment for them.

At the same time, he was uncertain of the consequences of the war and wished to ascertain the fate of his sons. Consequently, he asked Sanjay about the events at the battleground of Kurukshetra where the two armies had gathered. Sanjay was a disciple of Ved Vyas, and by the grace of his teacher, possessed the mystic ability of distant vision. Thus, he could see from afar all that transpired on the battleground and was giving Dhritarashtra a first-hand account of the events on the warfront.

अर्जुन उवाच ।
सेनयोरुभयोर्मध्ये रथं स्थापय मेऽच्युत ॥ 21 ॥

यावदेतान्निरीक्षेऽहं योद्धुकामानवस्थितान् ।
कैर्मया सह योद्धव्यमस्मिन् रणसमुद्यमे ॥ 22 ॥

arjuna uvācha
senayor ubhayor madhye ratham sthāpaya me 'chyuta

yāvadetān nirīkṣhe 'ham yoddhu-kāmān avasthitān
kairmayā saha yoddhavyam asmin raṇa-samudyame

Arjun said: O Infallible One, please take my chariot to the middle of both armies, so that I may look at the warriors arrayed for battle, whom I must fight in this great combat.

Arjun was a devotee of Shree Krishna, Who is the Supreme Lord of the entire creation. Yet, in this verse, Arjun instructed the Lord to drive his chariot to the desired spot. This directive reveals the sweetness of God's relationship with His devotees. Indebted by their love for Him, the Lord becomes the servant of His devotees. This is why He had consented to be Arjun's charioteer in the battle.

न काङ्क्षे विजयं कृष्ण न च राज्यं सुखानि च ।
किं नो राज्येन गोविन्द किं भोगैर्जीवितेन वा ॥ 32 ॥

येषामर्थे काङ्क्षितं नो राज्यं भोगाः सुखानि च ।
त इमेऽवस्थिता युद्धे प्राणांस्त्यक्त्वा धनानि च ॥ 33 ॥

na kāṅkṣhe vijayam kṛiṣhṇa na cha rājyam sukhāni cha
kim no rājyena govinda kim bhogairjīvitena vā

yeṣhām arthe kāṅkṣhitam no rājyam bhogāḥ sukhāni cha
ta ime 'vasthitā yuddhe prāṇāms tyaktvā dhanāni cha

O Krishna, I do not desire victory, kingdom, or the happiness accruing to it. Of what avail will be a kingdom, pleasures, or even life itself, when the very

persons for whom we covet them, are standing before us for battle?

Arjun's confusion arose from the fact that the act of killing is considered sinful; then to kill one's relatives seemed an even more grossly evil act. Even if he did engage in such a heartless act for the sake of the kingdom, Arjun felt that victory would not give him eventual happiness. He would be unable to share its glory with friends and relatives, whom he would have to slay to achieve this triumph.

Here, Arjun is displaying a lower set of sensibilities and confusing them for noble ones. From a spiritual perspective, indifference to worldly possessions and material prosperity is praiseworthy. But Arjun is not experiencing spiritual sentiments, rather his delusion is masquerading as compassion.

Virtuous sentiments bring internal harmony, satisfaction, and the joy of the soul. If Arjun's compassion was at the transcendental platform, he would have been elevated by the sentiment. But his experience is quite to the contrary—he is experiencing discord in his mind and intellect, and deep unhappiness within. The nature of these sentiments indicates his compassion is stemming from delusion.

अहो बत महत्पापं कर्तुं व्यवसिता वयम् ।
यद्राज्यसुखलोभेन हन्तुं स्वजनमुद्यताः ॥ 45 ॥

यदि मामप्रतीकारमशस्त्रं शस्त्रपाणयः ।
धार्तराष्ट्रा रणे हन्युस्तन्मे क्षेमतरं भवेत् ॥ 46 ॥

aho bata mahat pāpam kartum vyavasitā vayam
yad rājya-sukha-lobhena hantum sva-janam udyatāḥ

yadi mām apratīkāram ashastram shastra-pāṇayaḥ
dhārtarāṣhṭrā raṇe hanyus tan me kṣhemataram bhavet

Alas! How strange it is that we have set our mind to perform this great sin with horrifying consequences. Driven by the desire for kingly pleasures, we are intent on killing our own kinsmen. It would be better if, with weapons in hand, the sons of Dhritarashtra kill me unarmed and unresisting on the battlefield.

Arjun mentions a number of evils that would result from the impending battle, but he is unable to see that evil would actually prevail if these wicked people are allowed to thrive in society. He uses the word *aho* to express surprise. The word *bata* means 'horrible results'. Thus, Arjun is saying, 'How surprising it is that we have decided to commit sin by engaging in this war, even though we know of its horrifying consequences.'

Often, we blame circumstances or others but turn a blind eye to our weaknesses. Arjun's justification for not killing his greedy cousins and relatives was driven by his attachment towards them. He could not see that his compassion was not a transcendental sentiment but materialistic infatuation. It was based on the ignorance that one is the body.

The problem with Arjun's arguments was that he was using them to justify his delusion which had been created from his physical attachment, weakness of heart, and dereliction of duty. In the subsequent chapters, Shree Krishna explains the reasons why Arjun's arguments are untenable.

सञ्जय उवाच ॥
एवमुक्त्वार्जुनः सङ्ख्ये रथोपस्थ उपाविशत् ।
विसृज्य सशरं चापं शोकसंविग्नमानसः ॥ 47 ॥

sañjaya uvācha
evam uktvārjunaḥ saṅkhye rathopastha upāvishat
visṛijya sa-sharam chāpam shoka-samvigna-mānasaḥ

Sanjay said: Speaking thus, Arjun cast aside his bow and arrows, and sank into the seat of his chariot, his mind in distress and overwhelmed with grief.

Chapter 2

Sankhya Yog

The Yog of Analytical Knowledge

कार्पण्यदोषोपहतस्वभावः
पृच्छामि त्वां धर्मसम्मूढचेताः ।
यच्छ्रेयः स्यान्निश्चितं ब्रूहि तन्मे
शिष्यस्तेऽहं शाधि मां त्वां प्रपन्नम् ॥ 7 ॥

kārpaṇya-doṣhopahata-svabhāvaḥ
pṛichchhāmi tvām dharma-sammūḍha-chetāḥ
yach-chhreyaḥ syānnishchitam brūhi tanme
shiṣhyaste 'ham shādhi mām tvām prapannam

I am confused about my duty and am besieged with anxiety and faintheartedness. I am Your disciple and surrendered to You. Please instruct me for certain what is best for me.

This is a great moment in the Bhagavad Gita, when for the first time, Arjun, who is Shree Krishna's friend and cousin, requests Him to be his Guru. Arjun pleads to Shree Krishna that he has been overpowered by *kārpaṇya doṣh*, or the flaw of cowardice, so he requests the Lord to become his Guru and instruct him about the path to auspiciousness.

Shree Krishna states this Himself in the Bhagavad Gita in verse 4.34: 'Learn the Truth by approaching a spiritual master. Inquire from him with reverence and render service unto him. Such an enlightened saint can impart knowledge unto you because he has seen the Truth.'

Shree Krishna is in fact the first Guru of the world, because He is the Guru of Brahma, the first-born in this material world. In this verse, Arjun takes the step of surrendering to Jagadguru Shree Krishna as His disciple and requests Him for guidance regarding the proper course of action.

श्रीभगवानुवाच ।
अशोच्यानन्वशोचस्त्वं प्रज्ञावादांश्च भाषसे ।
गतासूनगतासूंश्च नानुशोचन्ति पण्डिताः ॥ 11 ॥

shrī bhagavān uvācha
ashochyān-anvashochas-tvam prajñā-vādānsh cha bhāṣhase
gatāsūn-agatāsūnsh-cha nānushochanti paṇḍitāḥ

The Supreme Lord said: While you speak words of wisdom, you are mourning for that which is not worthy of grief. The wise lament neither for the living nor for the dead.

Starting with this verse, Shree Krishna initiates His discourse with a dramatic opening statement. Arjun is lamenting for what he believes are very valid reasons. Rather than commiserate with him, Shree Krishna takes the wind out of his arguments. He says, 'Arjun, though you may feel you are speaking words of wisdom, you are actually talking and acting out of ignorance. No possible reason justifies lamentation. The pandits—those who are wise—never lament, neither for the living nor for the dead. Hence the grief you visualize in killing your relatives is illusory. And your misery proves you are not a pandit.'

देहिनोऽस्मिन्यथा देहे कौमारं यौवनं जरा ।
तथा देहान्तरप्राप्तिर्धीरस्तत्र न मुह्यति ॥ 13 ॥

dehino 'smin yathā dehe kaumāram yauvanam jarā
tathā dehāntara-prāptir dhīras tatra na muhyati

Just as the embodied soul continuously passes from childhood to youth to old age, similarly, at the time of death, the soul passes into another body. The wise are not deluded by this.

In the Vedic tradition, whenever divine knowledge is imparted, it usually begins with knowledge of the self. Shree Krishna follows the same approach in the Bhagavad Gita. He explains that the entity we call the 'self' is eternal.

With immaculate logic, Shree Krishna establishes the principle of transmigration of the soul from lifetime to lifetime. He explains that in one lifetime itself, we change bodies from childhood to youth to maturity and then to old age. In fact, modern science informs us that cells within the body undergo regeneration—old cells die, and new ones take their place. It is estimated that within seven years, all the cells of the body change. And yet, despite the continual change of the body, we perceive that we are the same person. This is because we are not the material body but the spiritual soul seated within.

In this verse, the word *deha* means 'the body', and *dehi* means 'possessor of the body', or the soul. Shree Krishna draws Arjun's attention to the fact that since the body is constantly changing in one lifetime itself, the soul passes through many bodies. Similarly, at the time of death, it passes into another body.

What we term as 'death' in worldly parlance is merely the soul discarding its old dysfunctional body, and what we call 'birth' is the soul taking on a new body elsewhere. This is the principle of reincarnation.

Without accepting the concept of rebirth, the disparity among human beings becomes inexplicable and irrational. For example, consider a man who is blind from birth. If that person asks why he was born handicapped, what logical answer can we give him? If we say it was the result of his karmas, he may argue that the present life is the only life he has, and therefore, there are no past karmas at the time of birth that should afflict him. If we say it was the will of God, it would also seem implausible, since God is all-merciful and would not unnecessarily bestow hardship on anyone. The only logical explanation is that the person was born blind as a consequence of karmas from past lives. As a result, from common sense and on the authority of the scriptures, we are obliged to believe in the concept of rebirth.

अन्तवन्त इमे देहा नित्यस्योक्ताः शरीरिणः ।
अनाशिनोऽप्रमेयस्य तस्माद्युध्यस्व भारत ॥ 18 ॥

antavanta ime dehā nityasyoktāḥ sharīriṇaḥ
anāshino 'prameyasya tasmād yudhyasva bhārata

Only the material body is perishable; the embodied soul within is indestructible, immeasurable, and eternal. Therefore, fight, O descendant of Bharat.

The gross body is made from mud. It is mud that gets converted to vegetables, fruits, grains, lentils, and grass. Cows graze the grass and produce milk. We humans consume these edibles, and they transform into our body. So, it is not an exaggeration to say that the body is created from mud.

At the time of death, when the soul departs, the body can have one of the three ends: *kṛimi*, *viḍ*, or *bhasma*. Either it is burnt, in which case it is converted to ashes and becomes mud. Or it is buried, in which case insects eat it and transform it into mud. Else, it is thrown into the river, in which case the aquatic creatures make it their fodder and excrete it as waste, which ultimately merges with the mud of the seabed.

In this manner, mud undergoes an amazing cycle in the world. It gets transformed into edibles, bodies are made from these edibles, and the bodies go back into mud. Shree Krishna tells Arjun, 'Within that material body is an eternal imperishable entity which is not made of mud. That is the divine soul, the real self.'

न जायते म्रियते वा कदाचि
नायं भूत्वा भविता वा न भूयः ।
अजो नित्यः शाश्वतोऽयं पुराणो
न हन्यते हन्यमाने शरीरे ॥ 20 ॥

na jāyate mriyate vā kadāchin
nāyam bhūtvā bhavitā vā na bhūyaḥ
ajo nityaḥ shāshvato 'yam purāṇo
na hanyate hanyamāne sharīre

The soul is neither born, nor does it ever die; nor having once existed, does it ever cease to be. The soul is without birth, eternal, immortal, and ageless. It is not destroyed when the body is destroyed.

वासांसि जीर्णानि यथा विहाय
नवानि गृह्णाति नरोऽपराणि ।
तथा शरीराणि विहाय जीर्णा
न्यन्यानि संयाति नवानि देही ॥ 22 ॥

vāsānsi jīrṇāni yathā vihāya
navāni gṛihṇāti naro 'parāṇi
tathā sharīrāṇi vihāya jīrṇānya
nyāni sanyāti navāni dehī

As a person sheds worn-out garments and wears new ones, likewise, at the time of death, the soul casts off its worn-out body and enters a new one.

नैनं छिन्दन्ति शस्त्राणि नैनं दहति पावकः ।
न चैनं क्लेदयन्त्यापो न शोषयति मारुतः ॥ 23 ॥

nainam chhindanti shastrāṇi nainam dahati pāvakaḥ
na chainam kledayantyāpo na shoṣhayati mārutaḥ

Weapons cannot shred the soul, nor can fire burn it. Water cannot wet it, nor can the wind dry it.

जातस्य हि ध्रुवो मृत्युर्ध्रुवं जन्म मृतस्य च ।
तस्मादपरिहार्येऽर्थे न त्वं शोचितुमर्हसि ॥ 27 ॥

jātasya hi dhruvo mṛityur dhruvam janma mṛitasya cha
tasmād aparihārye 'rthe na tvam shochitum arhasi

Death is certain for one who has been born, and rebirth is inevitable for one who has died. Therefore, you should not lament over the inevitable.

देही नित्यमवध्योऽयं देहे सर्वस्य भारत ।
तस्मात्सर्वाणि भूतानि न त्वं शोचितुमर्हसि ॥ 30 ॥

dehī nityam avadhyo 'yam dehe sarvasya bhārata
tasmāt sarvāṇi bhūtāni na tvam shochitum arhasi

O Arjun, the soul that dwells within the body is immortal; therefore, you should not mourn for anyone.

Often, in the course of His teachings, Shree Krishna explains a concept in a few verses and then states a verse summarizing those teachings. This verse is a synopsis of the instructions on the immortality of the self and its distinction from the body.

स्वधर्ममपि चावेक्ष्य न विकम्पितुमर्हसि ।
धर्म्याद्धि युद्धाच्छ्रेयोऽन्यत्क्षत्रियस्य न विद्यते ॥ 31 ॥

sva-dharmam api chāvekṣhya na vikampitum arhasi
dharmyāddhi yuddhāch chhreyo 'nyat kṣhatriyasya na vidyate

Besides, considering your duty as a warrior, you should

not waver. Indeed, for a warrior, there is no better engagement than fighting to uphold righteousness.

Here, Shree Krishna is encouraging Arjun to do his duty or *sva-dharma* which is to fight. *Sva-dharma* is one's duty as an individual in accordance with the Vedas.

There are two kinds of *sva-dharmas* or prescribed duties for the individual—*para dharma* or spiritual duties, and *apara dharma* or material duties. Considering oneself to be the soul, the prescribed duty is to love and serve God; this is called *para dharma*. The Vedas also prescribe duties for those who see themselves as the body—these are defined according to one's ashram (station in life) and varna (occupation) and are called *apara dharma* or mundane duties. This distinction between spiritual duties and material duties needs to be kept in mind while understanding the Bhagavad Gita and the Vedic philosophy at large.

अथ चेतत्त्वमिमं धर्म्यं संग्रामं न करिष्यसि ।
ततः स्वधर्मं कीर्तिं च हित्वा पापमवाप्स्यसि ॥ 33 ॥

atha chet tvam imam dharmyam sangrāmam na kariṣhyasi
tataḥ sva-dharmam kīrtim cha hitvā pāpam avāpsyasi

If, however, you refuse to fight this righteous war, abandoning your social duty and reputation, you will certainly incur sin.

If a warrior chooses to become non-violent on the battlefield, it will be dereliction of duty, and consequently, classified as a sinful act. This is why Shree Krishna states that if Arjun abandons his duty, considering it to be repugnant and troublesome, he will be committing a sin.

सुखदुःखे समे कृत्वा लाभालाभौ जयाजयौ ।
ततो युद्धाय युज्यस्व नैवं पापमवाप्स्यसि ॥ 38 ॥

sukha-duḥkhe same kṛitvā lābhālābhau jayājayau
tato yuddhāya yujyasva naivam pāpam avāpsyasi

Fight for the sake of duty, treating alike happiness and distress, loss and gain, victory and defeat. Fulfilling your responsibility in this way, you will never incur sin.

In verse 1.33, Arjun had expressed his fear that by killing his enemies he would incur sin. In verse 2.33, Shree Krishna explained that he would incur sin by not doing his duty of fighting this war. Arjun is caught in a paradox as it seems he will incur sin irrespective of whether he follows his *sva-dharma* or not. So, now Shree Krishna advises Arjun to do his duty without attachment to the fruits of his actions. Such an attitude to work will release him from any sinful reactions.

When we work with selfish motives, we create karmas which bring about their subsequent karmic reactions. We then get bound by the consequences of our actions. Bad deeds are obviously binding because we must reap their sinful consequences. However, it is important to note that mundane good deeds are also binding. They result in material rewards, which add to the stockpile of our karmas and thicken the illusion that there is happiness in the world.

If, however, we give up selfish motives, then our actions no longer create any karmic reactions. For example, murder is a sin, and the law of every country of the world declares it to be a punishable offence. But if a soldier kills an enemy soldier in battle, he is not penalized. In fact, he could even be awarded a medal for bravery. This is because his actions are not motivated by any ill-will or personal motive; they are performed as a matter of duty to the country. God's law is quite similar. If one gives up all selfish motives and works merely for the sake of duty towards the Supreme, then such work does not create any karmic reactions.

So, Shree Krishna advises Arjun to become detached from outcomes and simply focus on doing his duty. When he fights with equanimity—treating victory and defeat, pleasure and pain as the same—then despite killing his enemies, he will never incur sin.

कर्मण्येवाधिकारस्ते मा फलेषु कदाचन ।
मा कर्मफलहेतुर्भूर्मा ते सङ्गोऽस्त्वकर्मणि ॥ 47 ॥

karmaṇy-evādhikāras te mā phaleṣhu kadāchana
mā karma-phala-hetur bhūr mā te saṅgo 'stvakarmaṇi

You have a right to perform your prescribed duties, but you are not entitled to the fruits of your actions. Never consider yourself to be the cause of the results of your activities, nor be attached to inaction.

This is an extremely popular verse of the Bhagavad Gita. It offers deep insight into the proper spirit of work and is often quoted whenever the topic of *karm yog* is discussed. The verse gives the following four instructions regarding the science of work.

Do your duty, but do not concern yourself with the results. We must remember that our effort, not the results, is in our control. Several factors come into play to determine the overall results—destiny, our efforts, the will of God, the efforts of others, the cumulative karmas of the people involved, the place, the situation (luck), and so on. If we become anxious about the results, we will experience stress whenever they are not as per our expectations. So, Shree Krishna advises Arjun to give up concern for outcomes, and instead, focus solely on doing a good job. The fact is that when we are unconcerned about results, we can pay undivided attention to our efforts. And that is the best way to improve results.

The fruits of your actions are not for your enjoyment. To perform action is an integral part of human nature. Having come into this world, we all have various duties determined by our family situation, social position, occupation, and various responsibilities. While performing these actions, we must remember that we are not the enjoyers of the results; they are meant solely for the pleasure of God.

Material consciousness is characterized by the following manner of thoughts, 'I am the proprietor of all that I possess. All that is mine is meant for my enjoyment. I have the right to enhance my possessions and maximize my enjoyment.'

The reverse of this is spiritual consciousness, which is

characterized by thoughts, such as 'God is the owner and enjoyer of this entire world. I am merely His selfless servant. I must use all that I have in the service of God.' Along these lines, Shree Krishna instructs Arjun not to think of himself as the enjoyer of the fruits of his actions.

Give up the pride of doership even while working. Shree Krishna wants Arjun to give up *kartṛitvābhimān,* meaning 'the ego of being the doer'. He thus implies, 'O Gudakesh, neither harbour selfish motives in your work, nor consider yourself as the cause of the results.'

When we perform actions, why should we not consider ourselves as the doers? The reason is that our senses, mind, and intellect are inert; God energizes them with His power and puts them at our disposal. As a result, we can work only with the power received from Him.

If God did not supply our body-mind-soul mechanism the shakti to perform actions, we could not have done anything. Thus, we must accord all credit to Him, remembering that the power to do things comes from Him.

Do not be attached to inaction. Although the nature of living beings is to work, situations often arise where work seems burdensome and confusing. In such cases, instead of running away from it, we must enhance our wisdom, and then work in the right consciousness, as explained by Shree Krishna. Instead, considering work as loathsome and resorting to inaction is highly inappropriate. Becoming attached to inaction is never the solution and is clearly condemned by Shree Krishna.

श्रीभगवानुवाच ।
प्रजहाति यदा कामान्सर्वान्पार्थ मनोगतान् ।
आत्मन्येवात्मना तुष्टः स्थितप्रज्ञस्तदोच्यते ॥ 55 ॥

shrī bhagavān uvācha
prajahāti yadā kāmān sarvān pārtha mano-gatān
ātmany-evātmanā tuṣhṭaḥ sthita-prajñas tadochyate

The Supreme Lord said: O Parth, when one discards all selfish desires and cravings of the senses that torment the mind and becomes satisfied in the realization of the self, such a person is said to be transcendentally situated.

Previously Arjun had asked: O Keshav, what is the disposition of one who is situated in divine consciousness? How does an enlightened person talk? How does he sit? How does he walk? (2.54) Shree Krishna begins answering Arjun's questions here and continues on this topic till the end of the chapter.

Each fragment is naturally drawn towards its whole, just as a piece of stone is drawn by earth's gravitational pull towards it. The individual soul is a fragment of God, Who is infinite bliss. Hence, the soul experiences the natural urge for bliss. But in ignorance of its spiritual nature, it thinks of itself as the body and seeks to relish the bliss of the body from the world.

This world has been called *mṛiga tṛiṣhṇā* in the scriptures, meaning 'like the mirage seen by the deer'. The sun rays reflecting on the hot desert sand create an illusion of water for the deer. It thinks there is water ahead and runs to quench its thirst. But the closer it gets, the more the mirage fades away. Its dull intellect cannot recognize the illusion. The unfortunate deer keeps chasing the elusive water and dies of exhaustion on the desert sand. Similarly, the material energy, maya, too creates an illusion of happiness, and we run after it in the hope of quenching the thirst of our senses. But no matter how much we try, happiness keeps fading further away from us.

The simple truth is that our soul is divine, and it can only be satisfied by the divine bliss of God.

ध्यायतो विषयान्पुंसः सङ्गस्तेषूपजायते ।
सङ्गात्सञ्जायते कामः कामात्क्रोधोऽभिजायते ॥ 62 ॥

क्रोधाद्भवति सम्मोहः सम्मोहात्स्मृतिविभ्रमः ।
स्मृतिभ्रंशाद् बुद्धिनाशो बुद्धिनाशात्प्रणश्यति ॥ 63 ॥

dhyāyato viṣhayān pumsaḥ saṅgas teṣhūpajāyate
saṅgāt sañjāyate kāmaḥ kāmāt krodho 'bhijāyate

krodhād bhavati sammohaḥ sammohāt smṛiti-vibhramaḥ
smṛiti-bhranshād buddhi-nāsho buddhi-nāshāt praṇashyati

While contemplating on the objects of the senses, one develops attachment to them. Attachment leads to desire, and from desire arises anger.

Anger leads to clouding of judgement, which results in bewilderment of memory. When memory is bewildered, the intellect gets destroyed; and when the intellect is destroyed, one is ruined.

According to the Vedic scriptures, desire, anger, and greed are labelled as *manas rog* or diseases of the mind. In these two verses, Shree Krishna shares a perfect and penetrating insight into the functioning of the mind and the consequences of leaving these diseases unchecked.

When we repeatedly contemplate on the happiness we think we will get by acquiring something, our attachment to it grows. The greater the attachment, the greater the desire to obtain it. If the desire is fulfilled, it leads to greed; if the desire is unfulfilled, it results in anger.

When we are angry, all we are aware of is that our desire is not being fulfilled. Due to our attachment to get what we want, we lose our sense of right and wrong, the ability to discriminate, and we fail to bring the requisite knowledge to make an informed decision. In verse 3.38, Shree Krishna explains how knowledge is shrouded by desire during such moments. With our reptilian brain taking over and emotions surging high, this bewilderment of memory brings about destruction of the intellect. And when the intellect is destroyed, even momentarily, one loses sight of their internal moral compass. Needless to say, anger impairs judgement and one heads downhill.

रागद्वेषवियुक्तैस्तु विषयानिन्द्रियैश्चरन् ।
आत्मवश्यैर्विधेयात्मा प्रसादमधिगच्छति ॥ 64 ॥

rāga-dveṣha-viyuktais tu viṣhayān indriyaish charan
ātma-vashyair-vidheyātmā prasādam adhigachchhati

But one who controls the mind and is free from

attachment and aversion, even while using the objects of the senses, attains the grace of God.

The entire downward spiral leading to ruin begins with contemplating happiness in sense objects. The urge for happiness is as natural to the soul as thirst is to the physical body. It is impossible to think 'I will not contemplate happiness anywhere' because it is unnatural for the soul. The simple solution then is to envision happiness in the proper direction, i.e. in God. If we can repeatedly revise the thought that happiness is in God, we will develop attachment towards Him. This divine attachment does not degrade the mind like material attachment; rather, it purifies it. God is all-pure, and when we attach our mind to Him, the mind will also become pure.

Thus, whenever Shree Krishna asks us to give up attachment and desire, He is referring only to material attachment and desire. Spiritual attachment and desire are not to be given up; in fact, they are most praiseworthy. They are to be cultivated and increased for purification of the mind. The greater the burning desire we develop for God, the purer our mind will become. The jnanis who propound the worship of the undifferentiated attributeless Brahman do not understand this point when they recommend giving up all attachments. However, Shree Krishna states: 'Those who attach their minds to Me with unadulterated devotion rise above the three modes of material nature and attain the level of the supreme Brahman.' (14.26) He repeatedly urges Arjun to attach his mind to God in many verses ahead, such as 8.7, 8.14, 9.22, 9.34, 10.10, 11.54, 12.8, 18.55, 18.58, 18.65, etc.

Attachment (*raga*) and aversion (*dwesh*) are two sides of the same coin. Aversion is nothing but negative attachment. In attachment, the object of attachment repeatedly comes to one's mind; similarly, in aversion, the object of hatred keeps popping into the mind. So both attachment to material objects and aversion from them has the same effect on the mind—they dirty it and pull it into the three modes of material nature. When the mind is free from both *raga* and *dwesh* and is absorbed in devotion to God, one receives the grace of God and experiences his unlimited divine bliss. On experiencing that higher taste, the mind no longer feels attracted to the sense objects even while using them. Thus, even while tasting, touching, smelling, hearing, and seeing, the *sthita prajña* is free from both attachment and aversion.

या निशा सर्वभूतानां तस्यां जागर्ति संयमी ।
यस्यां जाग्रति भूतानि सा निशा पश्यतो मुनेः ॥ 69 ॥

yā nishā sarva-bhūtānām tasyām jāgarti sanyamī
yasyām jāgrati bhūtāni sā nishā pashyato muneḥ

What all beings consider as day is the night of ignorance for the wise, and what all creatures see as night is the day for the introspective sage.

Shree Krishna has used day and night figuratively here, so let us try and understand the true meaning. Those who are in mundane consciousness look to material enjoyment as the real purpose of life. They consider the opportunity for worldly pleasures as the success of life or 'day', and deprivation from sense pleasures as darkness or 'night'. On the other hand, those who have become wise with divine knowledge, see sense enjoyment as harmful for the soul, and hence, view it as 'night'. They consider refraining from the objects of the senses as elevating to the soul, and consequently look on it as 'day'. Using these connotations of the words, Shree Krishna states that what is 'night' for the sage is 'day' for the worldly-minded people and vice versa.

विहाय कामान्यः सर्वान्पुमांश्चरति निःस्पृहः ।
निर्ममो निरहङ्कारः स शान्तिमधिगच्छति ॥ 71 ॥

vihāya kāmān yaḥ sarvān pumānsh charati niḥspṛihaḥ
nirmamo nirahankāraḥ sa shāntim adhigachchhati

That person, who gives up all material desires and lives free from a sense of greed, proprietorship, and egoism, attains perfect peace.

In this verse, Shree Krishna lists the things that disturb one's peace and asks Arjun to give them up.

Chapter 3

Karm Yog

The Yog of Action

न कर्मणामनारम्भान्नैष्कर्म्यं पुरुषोऽश्नुते ।
न च संन्यसनादेव सिद्धिं समधिगच्छति ॥ 4 ॥

na karmaṇām anārambhān naiṣhkarmyam puruṣho 'shnute
na cha sannyasanād eva siddhim samadhigachchhati

One cannot achieve freedom from karmic reactions by merely abstaining from work, nor can one attain perfection of knowledge by mere physical renunciation.

The first line of this verse refers to the *karm yogi* (follower of the discipline of work), and the second line refers to the *sankhya yogi* (follower of the discipline of knowledge).

In the first line, Shree Krishna says that abstinence from work does not result in freedom from karmic reactions. The mind continues to engage in fruitive thoughts, and since mental work is also a form of karma, it also binds one in karmic reactions. A true *karm yogi* must learn to work without any attachment to the fruits of actions. This requires illumination of the intellect with wisdom. Hence, for success in karm yog, philosophic knowledge is necessary.

In the second line, Shree Krishna declares that the *sankhya yogi* cannot attain the state of knowledge merely by becoming a monk and renouncing the world. One might not hanker for the physical objects of the senses, but true knowledge cannot awaken as long as the mind remains impure.

The mind has a tendency to repeat its previous thoughts. Such repetition creates a channel within the mind, and new thoughts flow irresistibly in the same direction. Out of previous habit, the materially contaminated mind keeps running in the direction of anxiety, stress, resentment, and the whole gamut of material emotions. Thus, realized knowledge will not manifest in an impure heart through mere physical renunciation. It must be accompanied by suitable action that purifies the mind and intellect. Therefore, for success in *Sankhya Yog,* work is also necessary.

It is appropriately said that devotion without philosophy is sentimentality, and philosophy without devotion is intellectual speculation. Likewise, action and knowledge are necessary in both *Karm Yog* and *Sankhya Yog*. It is only their proportion that varies, thereby creating a difference between the two paths.

यस्त्विन्द्रियाणि मनसा नियम्यारभतेऽर्जुन ।
कर्मेन्द्रियैः कर्मयोगमसक्तः स विशिष्यते ॥ 7 ॥

yas-tvindriyāṇi manasā niyamyārabhate 'rjuna
karmendriyaiḥ karma-yogam asaktaḥ sa vishiṣhyate

But those karm yogis who control their knowledge senses with the mind, O Arjun, and engage the working senses

in working without attachment, are certainly superior.

The word karm yog has been used in this verse. It consists of two main concepts: *Karm* (occupational duties) and *Yog* (union with God). Hence, a karm yogi is one who performs worldly duties while keeping the mind attached to God. Such a karm yogi is not bound by karma even while performing all kinds of work. This is because what binds one to the Law of Karma is not actions, but the attachment to its fruits. And a true karm yogi is detached from outcomes. On the other hand, false renunciants gives up action but not attachment; thus, they remain bound by the Law of Karma.

Here, Shree Krishna says that those in household life who practise karm yog are superior to the false renunciants who continue to dwell on sense objects in their mind.

नियतं कुरु कर्म त्वं कर्म ज्यायो ह्यकर्मणः ।
शरीरयात्रापि च ते न प्रसिद्ध्येदकर्मणः ॥ 8 ॥

niyatam kuru karma tvam karma jyāyo hyakarmaṇaḥ
sharīra-yātrāpi cha te na prasiddhyed akarmaṇaḥ

You should thus perform your prescribed Vedic duties, since action is superior to inaction. By ceasing activity, even your bodily maintenance will not be possible.

Until the mind and intellect reach a state where they are absorbed in God-consciousness, physical work performed in an attitude of duty is very beneficial for one's internal purification. Hence, the Vedas prescribe duties for humans to help them discipline their mind and senses. In fact, laziness is one of the biggest pitfalls on the spiritual path.

Even the elementary physical activities of eating, bathing, and maintaining proper health require work. These obligatory actions are called *nitya karm*. To neglect these basic sustenance activities is not a sign of progress, but an indication of sloth, leading to emaciation and weakness of both body and mind. On the other hand, a cared for and nourished body is a positive adjunct on the road to spirituality. Inertia does not lend itself either to material or spiritual achievement. For the progress of our own soul, we must embrace duties that help elevate and purify our consciousness.

यज्ञार्थात्कर्मणोऽन्यत्र लोकोऽयं कर्मबन्धनः ।
तदर्थं कर्म कौन्तेय मुक्तसङ्गः समाचर ॥ 9 ॥

yajñārthāt karmaṇo 'nyatra loko 'yam karma-bandhanaḥ
tad-artham karma kaunteya mukta-saṅgaḥ samāchara

Work must be done as a yajna (sacrifice) to the Supreme Lord, otherwise, it causes bondage in this material world. Therefore, O son of Kunti, for the satisfaction of God, perform your prescribed duties without being attached to the results.

A knife in the hands of a robber is a weapon for intimidation or committing murder, but in the hands of a surgeon, is an invaluable instrument used for saving people's lives. The knife in itself is neither murderous nor benedictory—its effect is determined by how it is used. As Shakespeare said: 'There is nothing either good or bad but thinking makes it so.'

Similarly, work in itself is neither good nor bad. Depending upon the state of our mind, it can be either binding or elevating. Work done for pleasing our senses and satisfying our ego causes bondage to the material realm, while work performed as yajna for the pleasure of the Supreme Lord attracts divine grace and liberates us from maya. Since performing actions is our nature, we are forced to work in one of these two modes. We cannot remain without working as our mind cannot remain still.

If we do not perform actions as a sacrifice to God, we will be forced to work to gratify our mind and senses. Instead, when we perform work as a sacrifice, we then look upon the whole world and everything in it as belonging to God. As a result, serving Him becomes the only intention behind our works.

The Bhagavatam states in verse 4.30.19: 'The perfect karm yogis, even while fulfilling their household duties, do all their works as yajna to Me, knowing Me to be the Enjoyer of all activities. They spend whatever free time they have in hearing and chanting My glories. Such people, though living in the world, never get bound by their actions.'

मयि सर्वाणि कर्माणि संन्यस्याध्यात्मचेतसा ।
निराशीर्निर्ममो भूत्वा युध्यस्व विगतज्वरः ॥ 30 ॥

mayi sarvāṇi karmāṇi sannyasyādhyātma-chetasā
nirāshīr nirmamo bhūtvā yudhyasva vigata-jvaraḥ

Performing all works as an offering unto Me, constantly meditate on Me as the Supreme. Become free from desire and selfishness, and with your mental grief departed, fight!

In His typical style, Shree Krishna expounds on a topic and then finally presents the summary. The words *adhyātma chetasā* mean 'with thoughts resting on God'; *sannyasya* means 'renouncing all activities that are not dedicated to Him'; *nirāshīḥ* means 'without hankering for the results of the actions'. The *Krishnarpan bhav,* or 'sentiment of dedicating all actions to God', requires forsaking claim to proprietorship and renouncing desires for personal gain, hankering, and lamentation.

The summary of the instructions in the previous verses is that one should very faithfully reflect, 'My soul is a tiny part of the Supreme Lord Shree Krishna. He is the Enjoyer and Master of all. All my works are meant for His pleasure, and therefore, I will do my duties in the spirit of sacrifice to Him. Moreover, God supplies the energy by which I accomplish works of yajna. Thus, I should not take credit for my works.'

श्रेयान्स्वधर्मो विगुण: परधर्मात्स्वनुष्ठितात् ।
स्वधर्मे निधनं श्रेय: परधर्मो भयावह: ॥ 35 ॥

shreyān sva-dharmo viguṇaḥ para-dharmāt sv-anuṣhṭhitāt
sva-dharme nidhanam shreyaḥ para-dharmo bhayāvahaḥ

It is far better to perform one's natural prescribed duty, though tinged with faults, than to perform

another's prescribed duty, though perfectly. In fact, it is preferable to die in the discharge of one's duty, than to follow the path of another, which is fraught with danger.

In this verse, the word dharma has been used four times. Dharma is a word commonly used in Hinduism and Buddhism. But it is the most elusive word to translate into the English language. Terms, such as righteousness, good conduct, duty, and noble quality, among others, only describe an aspect of its meaning. Dharma comes from the root word *dhṛi*, which means *ḍhāraṇ karane yogya* or 'responsibilities, duties, thoughts, and actions that are appropriate for us'. For example, dharma of the soul is to love God. It is the central law of our being.

The prefix *sva* means 'the self'. Thus, sva-dharma is our personal dharma, which is the dharma applicable to our context, situation, maturity, and profession in life. This sva-dharma can change as our context in life changes and as we grow spiritually. By asking Arjun to follow his sva-dharma, Shree Krishna is telling him to follow his profession and not change it because someone may be doing something else.

It is more enjoyable to be ourself than to pretend to be someone else. The duties born of our nature can be easily performed with stability of mind. The duties of others may seem attractive from a distance and we may think of switching, but it is a risky thing to do. If they conflict with our nature, they will create disharmony in our senses, mind, and intellect. This will be detrimental for our consciousness and will hinder our progress on the spiritual path. Shree Krishna emphasizes this point dramatically by saying that it is better to die in the faithful performance of one's duty than to be in the unnatural position of doing another's duty.

धूमेनाव्रियते वह्निर्यथादर्शो मलेन च ।
यथोल्बेनावृतो गर्भस्तथा तेनेदमावृतम् ॥ 38 ॥

dhūmenāvriyate vahnir yathādarsho malena cha
yatholbenāvṛito garbhas tathā tenedam āvṛitam

Just as a fire is covered by smoke, a mirror is masked by dust, and an embryo is concealed by the womb, similarly one's knowledge gets shrouded by desire.

Knowledge of what is right or wrong is called discrimination and it resides in the intellect. However, desire is such a formidable adversary that it clouds the discriminatory ability of the intellect. Shree Krishna gives three grades of examples to illustrate this principle. Fire, which is the source of light, gets covered by smoke. This partial obscuring is like a thin cloud that sattvic desires create. A mirror, which is naturally reflective, gets obscured by dust. This semi-opacity is like the masking impact of rajasic desires on the intellect. And an embryo gets concealed in the womb. This complete obfuscation is like the consequence of tamasic desires subverting the power of discrimination. Similarly, in proportion to the grade of our desires, the spiritual knowledge we may have heard and read gets shrouded.

इन्द्रियाणि पराण्याहुरिन्द्रियेभ्यः परं मनः ।
मनसस्तु परा बुद्धिर्यो बुद्धेः परतस्तु सः ॥ 42 ॥

एवं बुद्धेः परं बुद्ध्वा संस्तभ्यात्मानमात्मना ।
जहि शत्रुं महाबाहो कामरूपं दुरासदम् ॥ 43 ॥

indriyāṇi parāṇyāhur indriyebhyaḥ param manaḥ
manasas tu parā buddhir yo buddheḥ paratas tu saḥ

evam buddheḥ param buddhvā sanstabhyātmānam ātmanā
jahi shatrum mahā-bāho kāma rūpam durāsadam

The senses are superior to the gross body, and superior to the senses is the mind. Beyond the mind is the intellect, and even beyond the intellect is the soul.

Thus, knowing the soul to be superior to the material intellect, O mighty armed Arjun, subdue the lower self (senses, mind, and intellect) by the higher self (strength of the soul), and kill this formidable enemy called desire.

An inferior entity can be controlled by its superior entity. Shree Krishna explains the gradation of superiority amongst the instruments God has provided to us. He describes that the body is made of gross matter; superior to it are the five knowledge-bearing senses (which grasp the perceptions of taste, touch, sight, smell, and sound); beyond the senses is the mind; superior to the mind is the intellect, with its ability to discriminate; but even beyond the intellect is the divine soul.

In conclusion, Shree Krishna emphasizes that we should slay this enemy called desire through knowledge of the self. Since the soul is a part of God, it is divine in nature. Thus, the divine bliss it seeks can only be attained from a divine subject, while the objects of the world are all material. These material objects can never fulfil the innate longing of the soul, so it is futile to create desires for them. We must exert and train the intellect to think in this manner, and then use it to control the mind and the senses.

Chapter 4

Jnana Karm Sanyas Yog

The Yog of Knowledge and the Disciplines of Action

स एवायं मया तेऽद्य योगः प्रोक्तः पुरातनः ।
भक्तोऽसि मे सखा चेति रहस्यं ह्येतदुत्तमम् ॥ 3 ॥

sa evāyam mayā te 'dya yogaḥ proktaḥ purātanaḥ
bhakto 'si me sakhā cheti rahasyam hyetad uttamam

The same ancient knowledge of Yog, which is the supreme secret, I am today revealing unto you, because you are My friend as well as My devotee, who can understand this transcendental wisdom.

Shree Krishna tells Arjun that the ancient science being imparted to him is an uncommonly known secret. Secrecy in the world is maintained for two reasons: either due to selfishness in keeping the truth to oneself or to protect the truth from the abuse of knowledge. The science of Yog remains a secret, not for either of these reasons, but because it requires a qualification to be understood. That qualification is revealed in this verse as devotion. The deep message of the Bhagavad Gita is not amenable to being understood merely through scholasticism or mastery of the Sanskrit language. It requires devotion, which destroys the subtle envy of the soul towards God and enables us to accept the humble position as His tiny parts and servitors.

Without a devotional heart, one cannot truly grasp the message of the Bhagavad Gita. This verse also invalidates the commentaries on the Bhagavad Gita written by scholars, jnanis, yogis, tapasvis, and many others, who lack bhakti towards God. According to this verse, since they are not devotees, they cannot comprehend the true import of the supreme science that was revealed to Arjun, and hence, their commentaries are inaccurate and/or incomplete.

यदा यदा हि धर्मस्य ग्लानिर्भवति भारत ।
अभ्युत्थानमधर्मस्य तदात्मानं सृजाम्यहम् ॥ 7 ॥

yadā yadā hi dharmasya glānir bhavati bhārata
abhyutthānam adharmasya tadātmānam sṛijāmyaham

Whenever there is a decline in righteousness and an increase in unrighteousness, O Arjun, at that time, I manifest Myself on earth.

Dharma is verily the prescribed actions, thoughts, values, and beliefs that are conducive to our spiritual growth and progress; the reverse of this is *adharma*, meaning unrighteousness. When unrighteousness prevails, the Creator and Administrator of the world intervenes by manifesting and re-establishing dharma. Such a descension of God is called an Avatar.

परित्राणाय साधूनां विनाशाय च दुष्कृताम् ।
धर्मसंस्थापनार्थाय सम्भवामि युगे युगे ॥ 8 ॥

paritrāṇāya sādhūnām vināshāya cha duṣhkṛitām
dharma-sansthāpanārthāya sambhavāmi yuge yuge

To protect the righteous, to annihilate the wicked, and to re-establish the principles of dharma, I appear on this earth, age after age.

Having stated in the last verse that God descends in the world, He now states three reasons for doing so: 1) To annihilate the wicked. 2) To protect the pious. 3) To establish dharma. However, if we study them closely, none of the three reasons seem truly convincing.

To protect the righteous. God is seated in the hearts of His devotees and always protects them from within. There is no need to take an Avatar for this purpose.

To annihilate the wicked. God is all-powerful and can kill the wicked merely by wishing it. Why does He need to take an Avatar to accomplish this?

To establish dharma. Dharma is eternally described in the Vedas. God can re-establish it through a Saint; He does not need to descend in His personal form to accomplish this.

How then can we make sense of the reasons that have been stated in this verse? Let's delve a little deeper to grasp the import of what Shree Krishna is saying.

The biggest dharma that the soul can engage in is devotion to God. That is what God strengthens by taking an Avatar. When He descends on earth, He reveals His divine forms, names, virtues, pastimes, abodes, and associates. This provides the souls with an easy basis for devotion. The formless aspect of God is very difficult to worship because the mind needs a form to focus upon and to connect with. On the other hand, devotion to the personal form of God is easy for people to understand, simple to perform, and pleasing to engage in.

rām eka tāpasa tiya tārī,

nāma koṭi khala kumati sudhārī

The *Ramcharitmanas* states that during His leelas on earth, Lord Ram helped only one Ahalya (Sage Gautam's wife, whom the Lord released from the body of a stone). However, since then, by chanting the divine name 'Ram', innumerable fallen souls have elevated themselves. So, a deeper understanding of this verse is:

To establish dharma. God descends to reinforce the dharma of devotion by revealing His names, forms, pastimes, virtues, abodes, and associates with the help of which souls may engage in bhakti and purify their mind.

To kill the wicked. Along with God, some liberated saints descend and pretend to be miscreants, to help facilitate His divine pastimes. For example, Ravan and Kumbhakarn were Jaya and Vijaya who came from the divine abode of God. They pretended to be demons and fought with Ram. They could not have been killed by anyone else, since they were divine personalities. So, God slayed such demons as a part of His leelas. And having killed them, He sent them to His divine abode from where they had originally come.

To protect the righteous. Many souls had become sufficiently elevated in their sadhana (spiritual practice) and had qualified to meet God face-to-face. When Shree Krishna descended in the world, these eligible souls obtained their first opportunity to participate in the Lord's divine pastimes. For example, some gopis (cowherd women of Vrindavan) were liberated souls from the divine abode who had come to assist in Shree Krishna's leelas. Other gopis were materially bound souls who were awarded their first chance to meet and serve God and participate in His leelas. So, when Shree Krishna descended in the world, such qualified souls got the opportunity to perfect their devotion by participating in His pastimes.

This is the deeper meaning of the verse. However if someone wishes to take the simpler meaning, it is not wrong either.

जन्म कर्म च मे दिव्यमेवं यो वेत्ति तत्त्वतः ।
त्यक्त्वा देहं पुनर्जन्म नैति मामेति सोऽर्जुन ॥ 9 ॥

janma karma cha me divyam evam yo vetti tattvataḥ
tyaktvā deham punar janma naiti mām eti so 'rjuna

Those who understand the divine nature of My birth and activities, O Arjun, upon leaving the body, do not have to take birth again but come to My eternal abode.

Our mind gets cleansed by engaging in devotional remembrance of the Supreme. This *smaran* can either be of the formless aspect of God or of His personal form.

For most people, devotion towards the formless seems inaccessible and nebulous as they find nothing tangible to feel connected with. On the other hand, devotion to the personal form of the Lord is simple and easily doable.

Such devotion requires harbouring divine sentiments towards God. For example, to do bhakti of Shree Krishna, we must cultivate divine feelings towards His names, forms, virtues, pastimes, abodes, and associates. Sublime sentiments purify our mind, even if harboured towards a stone deity. In this verse, Shree Krishna emphasizes the need for divine sentiments towards His pastimes.

To develop such bhav, we must understand the difference between God's actions and ours. We materially bound souls have not yet attained divine bliss, and hence, the longing of our soul is not yet satiated. Thus, our actions are motivated by the desire for personal fulfilment. However, God's actions have no personal motive because He is perfectly satiated by His own bliss. Therefore, whatever He does is for the welfare of the materially conditioned souls. Such divine actions that God displays are termed as 'leelas' while the actions we do are called 'work'.

Similarly, God's birth is also divine. Unlike ours, it does not take place physically from a woman.

If we can develop faith in the divinity of His pastimes and birth, then we will be able to easily engage in devotion to His personal form and attain the supreme destination.

ये यथा मां प्रपद्यन्ते तांस्तथैव भजाम्यहम् ।
मम वर्त्मानुवर्तन्ते मनुष्याः पार्थ सर्वशः ॥ 11 ॥

ye yathā mām prapadyante tāns tathaiva bhajāmyaham
mama vartmānuvartante manuṣhyāḥ pārtha sarvashaḥ

In whatever way people surrender unto Me, I reciprocate accordingly. Everyone follows My path, knowingly or unknowingly, O son of Pritha.

Here, Lord Krishna states that He reciprocates with everyone as they surrender to Him. For those who deny the existence of God, He meets them in the form of the Law of Karma—He sits inside their hearts, notes their actions, and dispenses the results. But such atheists also cannot get away from serving Him; they are obliged to serve God's material energy because maya, in its various apparitions, such as wealth, luxuries, relatives, prestige, etc., holds them under the sway of desire, anger, and greed. On the other hand, for those who turn their mind away from worldly attractions and look upon God as their only goal and refuge, He takes care of them just as a mother takes care of her child.

Shree Krishna uses the word *bhajāmi* which means 'to serve'. He serves the surrendered souls by destroying their accumulated karmas of endless lifetimes, cutting the bonds of maya, removing the darkness of material existence, and bestowing divine bliss, divine knowledge, and divine love. And when the devotee learns to love God selflessly, He willingly enslaves Himself to their love. In this way, God reciprocates with everyone as they surrender to Him.

कर्मणो ह्यपि बोद्धव्यं बोद्धव्यं च विकर्मण: ।
अकर्मणश्च बोद्धव्यं गहना कर्मणो गति: ॥ 17 ॥

karmaṇo hyapi boddhavyam boddhavyam cha vikarmaṇaḥ
akarmaṇash cha boddhavyam gahanā karmaṇo gatiḥ

You must understand the nature of all three—recommended action, wrong action, and inaction. The truth about these is profound and difficult to understand.

Work has been divided by Shree Krishna into three categories as follows:

Action. *Karm* is auspicious action recommended by the scriptures for regulating the senses and purifying the mind.

Forbidden action. *Vikarm* is inauspicious action prohibited by the scriptures since it is detrimental and results in degradation of the soul.

Inaction. *Akarm* is action that is performed without attachment to the results, merely for the pleasure of God. It neither has any karmic reactions and nor does it entangle the soul.

कर्मण्यकर्म य: पश्येदकर्मणि च कर्म य: ।
स बुद्धिमान्मनुष्येषु स युक्त: कृत्स्नकर्मकृत् ॥ 18 ॥

karmaṇyakarma yaḥ pashyed akarmaṇi cha karma yaḥ
sa buddhimān manuṣhyeṣhu sa yuktaḥ kṛitsna-karma-kṛit

Those who see action in inaction and inaction in action are truly wise amongst humans. Although performing

all kinds of actions, they are yogis and masters of all their actions.

Action in inaction. There is one kind of inaction where persons look upon their social duties as burdensome and renounce them out of indolence. While they physically give up actions, their mind continues to contemplate upon the objects of the senses. Such persons may appear to be inactive, but their lethargic idleness is actually sinful action. When Arjun suggested that he wished to shy away from his duty of fighting the war, Shree Krishna explained that doing so would be a sin, and he would go to the hellish regions for it.

Inaction in action. There is another kind of inaction performed by karm yogis. They execute their social duties without attachment to results, dedicating the fruits of their actions to God. Although engaged in all kinds of activities, they are not entangled in karmic reactions since they have no motive for personal enjoyment. There were many great kings in Indian history—Dhruv, Prahalad, Yudhishthir, Prithu, and Ambarish—who discharged their kingly duties to the best of their abilities, and yet, because their mind was not entangled in material desires but in God alone, their actions were termed *akarm* or inaction. Another name for *akarm* is karm yog.

तद्विद्धि प्रणिपातेन परिप्रश्नेन सेवया ।
उपदेक्ष्यन्ति ते ज्ञानं ज्ञानिनस्तत्त्वदर्शिनः ॥ 34 ॥

tad viddhi praṇipātena pariprashnena sevayā
upadekṣhyanti te jñānam jñāninas-tattva-darshinaḥ

Learn the Truth by approaching a spiritual master. Inquire from him with reverence and render service unto him. Such an enlightened saint can impart knowledge unto you because he has seen the Truth.

How can we obtain spiritual knowledge? Shree Krishna gives the answer in this verse. He says: 1) Approach a spiritual master. 2) Inquire from him submissively. 3) Render service to him.

The Absolute Truth cannot be understood merely by our own contemplation. In verse 11.22.10, the Bhagavatam states: 'The intellect of the soul is clouded by ignorance from endless lifetimes. Covered with nescience, the intellect cannot overcome its ignorance simply by its own effort. One needs to receive knowledge from a God-realized saint who knows the Absolute Truth.'

One of the most magnanimous graces of God is when He brings the soul in contact with a true guru. But the process of transfer of spiritual knowledge from the teacher to the student is very different from that of material knowledge. Secular education does not require deep respect for the teacher. The transmission of knowledge can be purchased simply by paying the teacher's fees. However, spiritual edification is neither imparted to the student by a mechanical teaching process, nor is it purchased for a price. It is revealed in the heart of the disciple by the Guru's grace, when the disciple develops humility and the Guru is pleased with the service attitude of the disciple.

अपि चेदसि पापेभ्य: सर्वेभ्य: पापकृत्तम: ।
सर्वं ज्ञानप्लवेनैव वृजिनं सन्तरिष्यसि ॥ 36 ॥

api chedasi pāpebhyaḥ sarvebhyaḥ pāpa-kṛit-tamaḥ
sarvam jñāna-plavenaiva vṛijinam santariṣhyasi

Even those who are considered the most immoral of all sinners can cross over this ocean of material existence by seating themselves in the boat of divine knowledge.

Material existence is like a vast ocean, in which one is tossed around by the waves of birth, disease, old age, and death. The material energy subjects everyone to three-fold miseries: *ādiātmik*—miseries due to one's own body and mind, *ādibhautik*—miseries due to other living entities, and *ādidaivik*—miseries due to environmental conditions. In this state of material bondage, there is no respite for the soul, and endless lifetimes have been subjected to these conditions. Like a football being kicked around the field, the soul is elevated to the celestial abodes, dropped to the hellish planes of existence, and brought back to the earthly realm, according to its karmas of righteous or sinful deeds.

Divine knowledge provides the boat to cross over the material ocean. The ignorant perform karmas and get bound by them. Performing the same karmas as a yajna to God liberates the knowledgeable. Thus, knowledge becomes the means for cutting material bondage.

न हि ज्ञानेन सदृशं पवित्रमिह विद्यते ।
तत्स्वयं योगसंसिद्धः कालेनात्मनि विन्दति ॥ 38 ॥

na hi jñānena sadṛisham pavitramiha vidyate
tatsvayam yogasansiddhaḥ kālenātmani vindati

In this world, there is nothing as purifying as divine knowledge. One who has attained purity of mind through prolonged practice of Yog, receives such knowledge within the heart, in due course of time.

Knowledge has the power to purify, elevate, liberate, and unite a person with God. It is thus supremely sublime and pure. But a distinction needs to be made between two kinds of knowledge—theoretical information and practical realization.

There is one kind of knowledge that is acquired by reading the scriptures and hearing from the Guru. This theoretical information alone is insufficient. It is like someone memorizing a cookbook but never entering the kitchen—it does not help satiate one's hunger. Similarly, one may acquire theoretical knowledge on the topics of the soul, God, maya, karm, jnana, and bhakti from the Guru, but that by itself does not make a person God-realized. When one practises sadhana in accordance with the theory, it results in purification of the consciousness. Then, from within, one gets realization of the nature of the self and its relationship with God.

तस्मादज्ञानसम्भूतं हृत्स्थं ज्ञानासिनात्मनः ।
छित्त्वैनं संशयं योगमातिष्ठोत्तिष्ठ भारत ॥ 42 ॥

tasmād ajñāna-sambhūtam hṛit-stham jñānāsinātmanaḥ
chhittvainam sanśhayam yogam ātiṣhṭhottiṣhṭha bhārata

Therefore, with the sword of knowledge, cut asunder the doubts that have arisen in your heart. O scion of Bharat, establish yourself in karm yog. Arise, stand up, and take action!

The use of the word 'heart' does not imply the physical machine housed in the chest that pumps blood in the body. The Vedas state that one's physical brain resides in the head, but the subtle mind resides in the region of the heart. This is the reason why in love and hatred, one experiences pain in the heart. In this sense, the heart is the source of compassion, love, sympathy, and all the good emotions. So, when Shree Krishna mentions doubts that have arisen in the heart, He means doubts that have arisen in the mind, which is the subtle machine that resides in the region of the heart.

As Arjun's Spiritual Master, the Lord has imparted the knowledge of how to gain insightful wisdom from the practice of karm yog. He now advises Arjun to utilize both wisdom and faith to cleave out the doubts from his mind. Then, He gives the call to action and asks Arjun to rise up and do his duty in the spirit of karm yog.

Chapter 5

Karm Sanyas Yog

The Yog of Renunciation

श्रीभगवानुवाच ।
संन्यासः कर्मयोगश्च निःश्रेयसकरावुभौ ।
तयोस्तु कर्मसंन्यासात्कर्मयोगो विशिष्यते ॥ 2 ॥

shrī bhagavān uvācha
sannyāsaḥ karma-yogash cha niḥshreyasa-karāvubhau
tayos tu karma-sannyāsāt karma-yogo vishiṣhyate

The Supreme Lord said: Both the path of karm sanyas (renunciation of actions) and karm yog (working in devotion) lead to the supreme goal. But karm yog is superior to karm sanyas.

In this verse, Shree Krishna compares karm sanyas and karm yog. It is a very deep verse; so, let's understand it one word at a time.

A karm yogi is one who does both—spiritual and social duties. Social duties are done with the body while the mind is attached to God.

Karm sanyas is for elevated souls who have already risen beyond the bodily platform. A karm sanyasi is one who discards social duties due to complete absorption in God and engages entirely in the performance of spiritual duties (devotional service to God).

Those who practise karm sanyas do not consider themselves to be the body, and as a result, they do not feel obligated to discharge their physical duties. Such karm sanyasis dedicate their full time and energy to spirituality, while karm yogis are required to split their time between worldly and spiritual duties. The karm sanyasis can thus move much faster towards God while the karm yogis are encumbered with social duties.

However, in this verse, Shree Krishna extols karm yog beyond karm sanyas and recommends it to Arjun as the preferred path. This is because karm sanyasis are exposed to a danger. If, having renounced their duties they cannot absorb their mind in God, they are left neither here nor there. In India, there are a plethora of such sadhus, who feel they are detached and renounce the world, but their mind is not yet attached to God. Consequently, they do not experience the divine bliss of the spiritual path. Although wearing the saffron clothes of mendicants, they indulge in grossly sinful activities, such as smoking opium. Only the ignorant mistake their sloth as detachment from the world.

On the other hand, karm yogis do both—their worldly duties and spiritual practice. So, if their mind turns away from spirituality, at least they have their work to fall back upon. Karm yog is thus the safer path for most people, while karm sanyas is only to be pursued under the expert guidance of a Guru.

ज्ञेयः स नित्यसंन्यासी यो न द्वेष्टि न काङ्क्षति ।
निर्द्वन्द्वो हि महाबाहो सुखं बन्धात्प्रमुच्यते ॥ 3 ॥

jñeyaḥ sa nitya-sannyāsī yo na dveṣhṭi na kāṅkṣhati
nirdvandvo hi mahā-bāho sukham bandhāt pramuchyate

The karm yogis, who neither desire nor hate anything, should be considered always renounced. Free from all dualities, they are easily liberated from the bonds of material energy.

Karm yogis continue to discharge their worldly duties while internally practising detachment. They accept both positive and negative outcomes with equanimity, as the grace of God. The Lord has designed this world so beautifully that it makes us experience both happiness and distress for our gradual elevation. If we continue to lead our regular lives and tolerate whatever comes our way while happily doing our duty, the world naturally pushes us towards spiritual perfection.

यत्साङ्ख्यैः प्राप्यते स्थानं तद्योगैरपि गम्यते ।
एकं साङ्ख्यं च योगं च यः पश्यति स पश्यति ॥ 5 ॥

yat sāṅkhyaiḥ prāpyate sthānam tad yogair api gamyate
ekam sāṅkhyam cha yogam cha yaḥ pashyati sa pashyati

The supreme state that is attained by means of karm sanyas is also attained by working in devotion. Hence, those who see karm sanyas and karm yog to be identical, truly see things as they are.

In spiritual practice, the intention of the mind is what matters, not the external activities. One may be living in the holy land of Vrindavan, but if the mind contemplates eating rasgullas in Kolkata, one will be deemed to be living in Kolkata. Conversely, if a person lives amidst the hubbub of Kolkata and keeps the mind absorbed in the divine land of Vrindavan, he will get the benefit of residing there. All the Vedic scriptures state that our level of consciousness is determined by the state of our mind:

mana eva manuṣhyāṇām kāraṇam bandha mokṣhayoḥ

(*Panchadashi*)

'The mind is the cause of bondage, and the mind is the cause of liberation.'

Those who do not possess this spiritual vision see the external distinction between a karm sanyasi and a karm yogi and declare the karm sanyasi to be superior because of external renunciation. But those who are learned see that both the karm sanyasi and the karm yogi have absorbed their minds in God, and they both are identical in their internal consciousness.

कायेन मनसा बुद्ध्या केवलैरिन्द्रियैरपि ।
योगिन: कर्म कुर्वन्ति सङ्‍गं त्यक्त्वात्मशुद्धये ॥ 11 ॥

kāyena manasā buddhyā kevalair indriyair api
yoginaḥ karma kurvanti saṅgam tyaktvātma-śhuddhaye

The yogis, while giving up attachment, perform actions with their body, senses, mind, and intellect, only for the purpose of self-purification.

The yogis understand that pursuing material desires in the quest for happiness is as futile as chasing a mirage. Realizing this, they renounce selfish desires and perform all their actions for the pleasure of God, Who alone is the *bhoktāram yajña tapasām* (Supreme enjoyer of all activities). Now, Shree Krishna brings a new twist to *samarpan* (dedication of all work to God). He says the enlightened yogis perform their works for the purpose of purification. How then do the works get dedicated to God?

The fact is that God needs nothing from us. He is the Supreme Lord of everything that exists and is perfect and complete in Himself. What can a tiny soul offer to the Almighty God that He does not already possess? Hence, while making an offering to God, it is customary to say: *tvadiyam vastu govinda tubhyameva samarpitam* 'O God, I am offering Your item back to You.'

However, there is one activity that is in our hands and not in God's—purification of our own heart (mind and intellect). When we purify our heart and engage it in devotion to God, it pleases Him more than anything else. Keeping this in mind, great yogis make purification of their heart the foremost goal, not out of selfishness, rather, for the pleasure of God.

Our only everlasting asset is the purity that we achieve. It goes with us into the next life while all material assets get left behind. In the final analysis, the success and failure of our life is determined by the extent to which we manage to achieve *antah karan shuddhi*. With this perspective, elevated yogis welcome adverse circumstances because they use them as opportunities to cleanse the heart.

Thus, when purification of the heart is made the prime motive of actions, adversarial circumstances are welcomed as God-sent opportunities for further progress, and one remains equanimous in both success and failure. As we work for the pleasure of God, the heart gets cleansed; and as our inner apparatus gets purified, we naturally offer the results of all our actions to the Supreme Lord.

विद्याविनयसम्पन्ने ब्राह्मणे गवि हस्तिनि ।
शुनि चैव श्वपाके च पण्डिताः समदर्शिनः ॥ 18 ॥

vidyā-vinaya-sampanne brāhmaṇe gavi hastini
shuni chaiva shva-pāke cha paṇḍitāḥ sama-darshinaḥ

The truly learned, with the eyes of divine knowledge, see with equal vision a Brahmin, a cow, an elephant, a dog, and a dog-eater.

When we perceive things through the perspective of knowledge, it is called *prajñā chakṣhu* which means 'with the eyes of knowledge'. Shree Krishna uses the words *vidyā sampanne* to the same effect, but He also adds *vinaya*, meaning humbleness. The sign of divine knowledge is that it is accompanied by a sense of humility while shallow bookish knowledge is accompanied with the pride of scholarship.

Shree Krishna reveals in this verse how divine knowledge bestows a vision so different from physical sight. Endowed with knowledge, devotees see all living beings as souls who are fragments of God and are therefore divine in nature. The examples given by Shree Krishna are of diametrically contrasting species and life forms. A Vedic Brahmin who conducts worship ceremonies is respected, while a dog-eater is usually looked down upon as an outcaste; a cow is milked for human consumption, but not a dog; an elephant is used for ceremonial parades, while neither the cow nor the dog are. From the physical perspective, these species are sharp contrasts in the spectrum of life on our planet. However, a truly learned person endowed with spiritual knowledge sees them all as eternal souls, and consequently, views them with an equal eye.

The Vedas do not support the view that the Brahmins (priestly class) are of higher caste, while the Shudras (labour class) are of lower caste. The perspective of knowledge is that even though the Brahmins conduct worship ceremonies, the Kshatriyas administer society, the Vaishyas conduct business, and the Shudras engage in labour, yet they all are eternal souls, who are tiny parts of God, and therefore, alike.

Chapter 6

Dhyan Yog

The Yog of Meditation

श्रीभगवानुवाच ।
अनाश्रितः कर्मफलं कार्यं कर्म करोति यः ।
स संन्यासी च योगी च न निरग्निर्न चाक्रियः ॥ 1 ॥

shrī bhagavān uvācha
anāshritaḥ karma-phalam kāryam karma karoti yaḥ
sa sannyāsī cha yogī cha na niragnir na chākriyaḥ

The Supreme Lord said: Those who perform prescribed duties without desiring the results of their actions are actual sanyasis (renunciates) and yogis, not those who have merely ceased performing sacrifices, such as *Agnihotra Yajna* or abandoned bodily activities.

The ritualistic activities described in the Vedas include fire sacrifices, such as *Agnihotra Yajna*. The rules for those who enter the renounced order of sanyas state that they should not perform karm-kand activities. However, Shree Krishna states in this verse that merely giving up the sacrificial fire does not make one a sanyasi (renunciant).

Persons who perform karm yog do all activities in the spirit of humble service to God without any desire whatsoever for rewards. Even though they may be *grihasthas* (householders), such persons are true yogis and real renunciants.

यं संन्यासमिति प्राहुर्योगं तं विद्धि पाण्डव ।
न ह्यसंन्यस्तसङ्कल्पो योगी भवति कश्चन ॥ 2 ॥

yam sannyāsam iti prāhur yogam tam viddhi pāṇḍava
na hyasannyasta-saṅkalpo yogī bhavati kashchana

What is known as sanyas is non-different from Yog, for none become yogis without renouncing worldly desires.

A sanyasi is one who renounces pleasures of the mind and senses. But mere renunciation is not the goal, nor is it sufficient to reach the goal. Renunciation means that our running in the wrong direction has stopped, i.e. we are no longer aiming for worldly gratification. However, the destination is not reached just by stopping. The purpose of the soul's journey is God-realization. The process of going towards God—taking the mind towards Him—is the path of Yog. Those who have incomplete knowledge of the goal of life look upon renunciation as the highest goal of spirituality. On the other hand, those who truly understand the goal of life regard God-realization as the ultimate goal of their spiritual endeavours.

In the first line of this verse, Shree Krishna states that a real sanyasi (renunciant) is one who is a yogi, i.e. one whose mind is united with God in loving service. In the second line, Shree Krishna states that one cannot be a yogi without giving up material desires. If there are material desires in the mind, then it will naturally run towards the world. Since it is the mind that has to be united with God, this is only possible if the mind is free from all material desires. Thus, to be a yogi, one must be a sanyasi from within; and one can only be a sanyasi if one is a yogi.

उद्धरेदात्मनात्मानं नात्मानमवसादयेत् ।
आत्मैव ह्यात्मनो बन्धुरात्मैव रिपुरात्मनः ॥ 5 ॥

uddhared ātmanātmānam nātmānam avasādayet
ātmaiva hyātmano bandhur ātmaiva ripur ātmanaḥ

Elevate yourself through the power of your mind and not degrade yourself, for the mind can be the friend and also the enemy of the self.

We are responsible for our own elevation or debasement. Nobody can traverse the path of God-realization for us. Saints and Gurus show us the way, but we have to walk it ourselves.

We have had innumerable lifetimes, and enlightened saints have always been present on the earth. At any period of time, if the world is devoid of such Saints, then the souls of that period cannot become God-realized. How then can they fulfil the purpose of human life which is to attain the Supreme? For this reason, the Lord ensures that divine saints are always present to guide sincere seekers and inspire humanity. So, in infinite past lifetimes, we too must have met God-realized saints many times, and yet we did not become perfected souls. This means that the problem was not lack of proper guidance, but our reluctance in either accepting it or working in alignment with it. Before we can move forward, we must first accept responsibility for our present level of spirituality or lack thereof. Only then will we realize that since we brought ourselves to our present state, we can also elevate ourselves by our own efforts.

When we suffer reversals, we tend to hold others responsible and complain that they are our enemies. However, the biggest enemy is our own mind. Shree Krishna states that on the one hand, as the greatest benefactor of the soul, the mind has the potential to give us the most benefit; on the other hand, as our greatest adversary, it also has the potential for causing the utmost harm. A controlled mind can lift us to great heights, whereas an uncontrolled mind can degrade our consciousness with the most ignoble thoughts.

So, when Shree Krishna says that we must use the mind to elevate the self, He means we must use the higher mind (buddhi or intellect) to manage the lower mind (mana).

बन्धुरात्मात्मनस्तस्य येनात्मैवात्मना जितः ।
अनात्मनस्तु शत्रुत्वे वर्तेतात्मैव शत्रुवत् ॥ 6 ॥

bandhur ātmātmanas tasya yenātmaivātmanā jitaḥ
anātmanas tu shatrutve varte tātmaiva shatru-vat

For those who have conquered the mind, it is their friend. For those who have failed to do so, the mind works like an enemy.

We dissipate a large portion of our thought power and energy in combatting people whom we perceive as enemies and potentially harmful to us. The Vedic scriptures say the biggest enemies—lust, anger, greed, envy, illusion, and other negative emotions—reside in our own mind. These internal enemies are even more pernicious than the outer ones. The external demons may injure us for some time, but the demons sitting within our own mind have the ability to make us live in constant misery. We all know people who had everything favourable in the world but lived miserable lives because their mind tormented them incessantly through depression, hatred, tension, anxiety, and stress.

Vedic philosophy lays great emphasis on the ramification of thoughts. Illness is caused not only by viruses and bacteria but also by the negativities we harbour in the mind. If someone accidentally throws a stone at you, it may hurt for a few minutes, but by the next day, you probably would have forgotten about it. However, if someone says something unpleasant, it may continue to agitate your mind for years.

This shows the immense power of thoughts. When we nourish hatred in our mind, our negative thoughts do more damage to us than the object of our hatred. It has been very sagaciously stated: 'Resentment is like drinking poison and hoping that the other person dies.' The problem is that most people do not even realize that their own uncontrolled mind is causing them so much harm.

However, the same mind has the potential of becoming our best friend if we bring it under the control of the intellect through spiritual practice. The more powerful an entity is, the greater is the danger of its misuse, and also the greater is the scope for its utilization. Since the mind is such a powerful machine fitted into our bodies, it can work as a two-edged sword. Thus, those who slide to demoniac levels do so because of their mind, while those who attain sublime heights also do so because of their purified mind.

योगी युञ्जीत सततमात्मानं रहसि स्थितः ।
एकाकी यतचित्तात्मा निराशीरपरिग्रहः ॥ 10 ॥

yogī yuñjīta satatam ātmānam rahasi sthitaḥ
ekākī yata-chittātmā nirāshīr aparigrahaḥ

Those who seek the state of Yog should reside in seclusion, constantly engaged in meditation with a controlled mind and body, getting rid of desires and possessions for enjoyment.

To attain the state where the intellect rules the mind, Shree Krishna recommends meditation.

The first point He mentions is the need for a secluded place. All day long, we are usually surrounded by a worldly environment—these material activities, people, and conversations tend to make the mind more worldly. In order to elevate the mind towards God, we need to dedicate some time on a daily basis for secluded sadhana.

In our daily schedule, we can allocate some time for sadhana or spiritual practice, where we isolate ourselves in a room that is free from worldly disturbances. Shutting ourselves out from the world, we should do sadhana to purify the mind and solidify its focus on God. If we practise in this manner for one to two hours every day, we will reap its benefits all through the day even while engaged in worldly activities. In this manner we will be able to retain the elevated state of consciousness that was gathered during the daily sadhana in isolation from the world.

प्रशान्तात्मा विगतभीर्ब्रह्मचारिव्रते स्थितः ।
मनः संयम्य मच्चित्तो युक्त आसीत मत्परः ॥ 14 ॥

युञ्जन्नेवं सदात्मानं योगी नियतमानसः ।
शान्तिं निर्वाणपरमां मत्संस्थामधिगच्छति ॥ 15 ॥

prashāntātmā vigata-bhīr brahmachāri-vrate sthitaḥ
manaḥ sanyamya mach-chitto yukta āsīta mat-paraḥ

yuñjann evam sadātmānam yogī niyata-mānasaḥ
shāntim nirvāṇa-paramām mat-sansthām adhigachchhati

With a serene, fearless, and unwavering mind, and staunch in the vow of celibacy, the vigilant yogi should meditate on Me, having Me alone as the supreme goal.

Thus, constantly keeping the mind absorbed in Me, the yogi of disciplined mind attains nirvana and abides in Me in supreme peace.

A variety of meditation techniques exist in the world, such as Zen techniques, Buddhist techniques, Tantric techniques, Taoist techniques, Vedic techniques, and so on. In Hinduism itself, there are innumerable techniques. The million-dollar question is: which of these should we adopt for our personal practice? Shree Krishna states that the object of meditation should be God Himself and God alone.

The aim of meditation is not merely to enhance concentration and focus but also to purify the mind. Meditation on the breath, chakras, void, flame, and other items is helpful in developing focus. However, purification of the mind is only possible when we fix it upon an all-pure object, which is God Himself. Verse 14.26 states that God is beyond the three modes of material nature, and when one fixes the mind upon Him, it too rises above the three modes. Thus, while meditating upon the pranas may be called transcendental by its practitioners, true transcendental meditation is upon God alone.

Now, what is the way to focus the mind on God? We can make all aspects of God—His names, forms, virtues, pastimes, abodes, and associates—the objects of meditation. They all are non-different from God and replete with all His energies. Hence, devotees may meditate upon any of these and get the true benefit of meditating upon God.

The Ramayan states:

brahma rām teṅ nāmu baṛa, bara dāyaka bara dāni

'God's name is bigger than God Himself, in terms of its utility to the souls.' Taking His name is a very convenient way of remembering God, since it can be taken anywhere and everywhere—while walking, talking, sitting, eating, and any other activity we do.

For most sadhaks, His name by itself is not sufficiently attractive for enchanting the mind. Due to sanskars of endless lifetimes, the mind is naturally drawn to forms. Using the form of God as the foundation, meditation becomes natural and easy. This is called *Roop dhyan* meditation.

Once the mind is focused upon the form of God, we can then further enhance it by contemplating on the virtues of God—His compassion, beauty, knowledge, love, benevolence, grace, and so on. One can then advance in meditation by serving God in the mind. We can visualize ourselves offering food to Him, worshipping Him, singing to Him, massaging His feet, fanning Him, bathing Him, cooking for Him, and other services. This is called *Manasi seva* (serving God in the mind). In this way, we can meditate upon the names, forms, virtues, pastimes, abodes, and associates of God. All these become powerful means of fulfilling Shree Krishna's instruction to Arjun to keep the mind absorbed in Him.

At the end of the verse, Shree Krishna gives the ultimate benefits of meditation, which are liberation from maya and everlasting beatitude of God-realization.

नात्यश्नतस्तु योगोऽस्ति न चैकान्तमनश्नतः ।
न चाति स्वप्नशीलस्य जाग्रतो नैव चार्जुन ॥ 16 ॥

युक्ताहारविहारस्य युक्तचेष्टस्य कर्मसु ।
युक्तस्वप्नावबोधस्य योगो भवति दुःखहा ॥ 17 ॥

nātyashnatastu yogo 'sti na chaikāntam anashnataḥ
na chāti-svapna-shīlasya jāgrato naiva chārjuna

yuktāhāra-vihārasya yukta-cheṣhṭasya karmasu
yukta-svapnāvabodhasya yogo bhavati duḥkha-hā

O Arjun, those who eat too much or too little, sleep too much or too little, cannot attain success in Yog.

But those who are temperate in eating and recreation, balanced in work, and regulated in sleep, can mitigate all sorrows by practising Yog.

After describing the object of meditation and the end-goal achieved by it, Shree Krishna shares some regulations to follow. He states that those who break the rules of bodily maintenance cannot be successful in Yog. Often beginners on the path with their incomplete wisdom state: 'You are the soul and not this body. So simply engage in spiritual activity and forget about the maintenance of the body.'

However, such a philosophy cannot get one too far. It is true that we are not the body, yet the body is our carrier as long as we live, and we are obliged to take care of it. The Ayurvedic text *Charak Samhita* states: *śharīra mādhyaṁ khalu dharma sādhanam* 'The body is the vehicle for engaging in religious activity.' If the body becomes unwell, then spiritual pursuits get impeded too. Material science is necessary for the maintenance of our body, while spiritual science is necessary for the manifestation of the internal divinity within us. We must balance both in our life to reach the ultimate goal of God-realization. Hence, yogasans, pranayam, and the science of proper diet are an essential part of Vedic knowledge.

Yog is the union of the soul with God. The opposite of Yog is *bhog* which means engagement in sensual pleasures. Indulgence in *bhog* violates the natural laws of the body and results in *rog* (disease). If the body becomes diseased, it impedes the practice of Yog. Thus, in this verse, Shree Krishna states that by being temperate in physical activities and practising Yog, we can become free from the sorrows of the body and mind.

यत्रोपरमते चित्तं निरुद्धं योगसेवया ।
यत्र चैवात्मनात्मानं पश्यन्नात्मनि तुष्यति ॥ 20 ॥

सुखमात्यन्तिकं यत्तद्बुद्धिग्राह्यमतीन्द्रियम् ।
वेत्ति यत्र न चैवायं स्थितश्चलति तत्त्वतः ॥ 21 ॥

yatroparamate chittam niruddham yoga-sevayā
yatra chaivātmanātmānam pashyann ātmani tuṣhyati

sukham ātyantikam yat tad buddhi-grāhyam atīndriyam
vetti yatra na chaivāyam sthitash chalati tattvataḥ

When the mind, restrained from material activities, becomes still by the practice of Yog, then the yogi is able to behold the soul through the purified mind, and he rejoices in the inner joy.

In that joyous state of Yog, called samadhi, one experiences supreme boundless divine bliss, and thus situated, one never deviates from the Eternal Truth.

Through the practice of meditation, when one's mind is exclusively and continously focused on God, the subconscious mind becomes purified, and one is able to perceive the self as distinct from the body, mind, and intellect. For example, if there is muddy water in a glass, we cannot see through it. However, if we put alum in the water, the mud settles down and the water becomes clear. Similarly, when the mind is unclean, it obscures perception of the soul and any acquired scriptural knowledge of the atma is only at the theoretical level. But when the mind becomes pure, the soul is directly perceived through realization.

When the mind is in union with God, the soul experiences the ineffable and sublime bliss beyond the scope of the senses. This state is called samadhi in the Vedic scriptures.

In the state of samadhi, experiencing complete satisfaction and contentment, the soul has nothing left to desire, and becomes firmly situated in the Absolute Truth, without deviating from it at all.

यतो यतो निश्चरति मनश्चञ्चलमस्थिरम् ।
ततस्ततो नियम्यैतदात्मन्येव वशं नयेत् ॥ 26 ॥

yato yato nishcharati manash chañchalam asthiram
tatas tato niyamyaitad ātmanyeva vasham nayet

Whenever and wherever the restless and unsteady mind wanders, one should bring it back and continually focus it on God.

Success in meditation is not achieved in a day; the path to perfection is long and arduous. When we sit for meditation with the resolve to focus our mind on God, we will find that ever so often, it wanders off in worldly *saṅkalp* and *vikalp*. To deal with this, it becomes important to understand the three steps involved in the process of meditation:

- With the intellect's power of discrimination, we decide that the world is not our goal. So, we forcefully remove the mind from the world. This requires effort.
- Again, with the power of discrimination, we understand that God alone is ours, and God-realization is our goal. Now, we bring the mind to focus upon God. This also requires effort.
- The mind comes away from God and wanders back into the world. This does not require effort; it happens automatically.

When the third step happens by itself, sadhaks often become disappointed and lament, 'I tried so hard to focus upon God, but the mind went back into the world.' Shree Krishna advises us not to feel disappointed. He says the mind is fickle and wanders off despite our best efforts to control it. However, when it does drift away, we should once again repeat steps 1 and 2—take the mind away from the world and bring it back to God. Once again, we will experience that step 3 takes place by itself. We should not lose heart, and instead, repeat steps 1 and 2.

We will have to do this repeatedly. Then slowly, the mind's attachment towards God will start increasing. And simultaneously, its detachment from the world will also increase. As this happens, it will become easier and easier to meditate. But in the beginning, we must be prepared for the battle involved in disciplining the mind.

चञ्चलं हि मनः कृष्ण प्रमाथि बलवद्दृढम् ।
तस्याहं निग्रहं मन्ये वायोरिव सुदुष्करम् ॥ 34 ॥

chañchalam hi manaḥ kṛiṣhṇa pramāthi balavad dṛiḍham
tasyāham nigraham manye vāyor iva su-duṣhkaram

The mind is very restless, turbulent, strong, and obstinate, O Krishna. It appears to me that it is more difficult to control than the wind.

Arjun speaks for all of us when he describes the troublesome mind. It is restless because it keeps flitting in different directions, from subject to subject. It is turbulent because it creates upheavals in one's consciousness, in the form of hatred, anger, desire, greed, envy, anxiety, fear, attachment, and a host of other negativities. It is strong because it overpowers the intellect with its vigorous currents and destroys the faculty of discrimination. The mind is also obstinate because when it catches a harmful thought, it refuses to let go, and continues to ruminate over it again and again, even to the dismay of the intellect. Thus, enumerating its unwholesome characteristics, Arjun declares that the mind is even more difficult to control than the wind. It is a powerful analogy for no one can ever think of controlling the mighty wind in the sky.

श्रीभगवानुवाच ।
असंशयं महाबाहो मनो दुर्निग्रहं चलम् ।
अभ्यासेन तु कौन्तेय वैराग्येण च गृह्यते ॥ 35 ॥

shrī bhagavān uvācha
asanshayam mahā-bāho mano durnigraham chalam
abhyāsena tu kaunteya vairāgyeṇa cha gṛihyate

Lord Krishna said: O mighty-armed son of Kunti, what you say is correct; the mind is indeed very difficult to restrain. But by practice and detachment, it can be controlled.

Shree Krishna does not deny the problem by saying, 'Arjun, what nonsense are you speaking? The mind can be controlled very easily.' Rather, He agrees with Arjun's statement that the mind is indeed very difficult to control. However, so many things are difficult to achieve in the world, yet, we remain undaunted and move forward. For example, sailors know that the sea is dangerous for many reasons including terrible storms. And yet, they have never looked upon those dangers as sufficient reasons for remaining ashore. Here, Shree Krishna assures Arjun that the mind can be controlled by *vairāgya* and *abhyās*.

Vairāgya means detachment. Due to practice from previous endless lifetimes, the mind has become conditioned to running towards the objects of its attachment. Developing detachment eradicates the unnecessary wanderings of the mind.

Abhyās means practice or a concerted and persistent effort to change an old habit or develop a new one. In all fields of human endeavour, practice is the key that opens the door to mastery and excellence. The obstinate and turbulent mind has to be made to rest on the lotus feet of the Supreme Lord through *abhyās*. Take the mind away from the world—this is *vairāgya*—and bring the mind to rest on God—this is *abhyās*.

योगिनामपि सर्वेषां मद्गतेनान्तरात्मना ।
श्रद्धावान्भजते यो मां स मे युक्ततमो मतः ॥ 47 ॥

yogināṁ api sarveṣhām mad-gatenāntar-ātmanā
shraddhāvān bhajate yo mām sa me yuktatamo mataḥ

Of all yogis, those whose minds are always absorbed in Me, and who engage in devotion to Me with great faith, them I consider to be the highest of all.

Even among yogis, there are karm yogis, bhakti yogis, jnana yogis, ashtang yogis, and others. This verse puts to rest the debate about which form of Yog is the highest. Shree Krishna declares the bhakti yogi to be the highest, superior to even the best ashtang yogi and hatha yogi. That is because bhakti, or devotion, is the highest power of God. It is such a power that binds God and makes Him a slave of His devotee.

In this verse, Shree Krishna has used the word *bhajate*. It comes from the root word *bhaj* which means 'to serve'. It is a far more significant word for devotion than 'worship', which means 'to adore'. Here, Shree Krishna is talking about those who not only adore Him, but also serve Him with loving devotion. They are thus established in the natural position of the soul as the servant of God. The other kinds of yogis are still incomplete in their realization; they have connected themselves with God but are not yet situated in the understanding that they are His eternal servants.

Thus, the bhakti yogi possesses the power of divine love, is dearest to God, and is considered by Him to be the highest of all.

Chapter 7

Jnana Vijnana Yog

Yog through the Realisation of Divine Knowledge

श्रीभगवानुवाच ।
मय्यासक्तमनाः पार्थ योगं युञ्जन्मदाश्रयः ।
असंशयं समग्रं मां यथा ज्ञास्यसि तच्छृणु ॥ 1 ॥

shrī bhagavān uvācha
mayyāsakta-manāḥ pārtha yogam yuñjan mad-āshrayaḥ
asanshayam samagram mām yathā jñāsyasi tach chhṛiṇu

The Supreme Lord said: Now listen, O Arjun, how, with the mind attached exclusively to Me, and surrendering to Me through the practice of bhakti yog, you can know Me completely, free from doubt.

At the conclusion of chapter six, Shree Krishna had declared that those who devotedly serve Him, with mind focused exclusively on Him, are the best among all yogis. This statement leads to some questions: What is the way to know the Supreme Lord? How should we worship God? The Lord now begins to answer them.

ज्ञानं तेऽहं सविज्ञानमिदं वक्ष्याम्यशेषतः ।
यज्ज्ञात्वा नेह भूयोऽन्यज्ज्ञातव्यमवशिष्यते ॥ 2 ॥

jñānam te 'ham sa-vijñānam idam vakṣhyāmyasheṣhataḥ
yaj jñātvā neha bhūyo 'nyaj jñātavyam-avashiṣhyate

I shall now reveal unto you fully this knowledge and wisdom, knowing which, nothing else remains to be known in this world.

Knowledge acquired through the senses, mind, and intellect is called jnana. Knowledge that comes as an insight from within as a result of spiritual practice is called vijnana (wisdom). Vijnana is not intellectual knowledge; it is direct experiential realization. For example, we may hear about the sweetness of honey, but it remains theoretical knowledge. It is only when we taste the honey that we get experiential realization of its sweetness. Similarly, the theoretical knowledge we get from the Guru and the scriptures is jnana. And when we practise sadhana as per that knowledge, then the knowledge that awakens within us as realization is called vijnana.

Shree Krishna declares that He will illumine Arjun with the theoretical knowledge of the Supreme Divine Personality and help him gain the associated inner wisdom. On realization of this knowledge, nothing further remains to be known.

मनुष्याणां सहस्रेषु कश्चिद्यतति सिद्धये ।
यततामपि सिद्धानां कश्चिन्मां वेत्ति तत्त्वतः ॥ 3 ॥

manuṣhyāṇām sahasreṣhu kashchid yatati siddhaye
yatatām api siddhānām kashchin mām vetti tattvataḥ

Amongst thousands of persons, hardly one strives for perfection; and amongst those who have achieved perfection, hardly one knows Me in truth.

Why do souls who have achieved perfection in spiritual practices not know God in Truth? This is because it is not possible to know or perceive Him without bhakti. Spiritual aspirants who practise karm, jnana, Ashtang yog, or other techniques, without devotion cannot know God. Hence, their understanding is limited to the theoretical knowledge, and they are bereft of the associated vijnana.

भूमिरापोऽनलो वायुः खं मनो बुद्धिरेव च ।
अहङ्कार इतीयं मे भिन्ना प्रकृतिरष्टधा ॥ 4 ॥

bhūmir-āpo 'nalo vāyuḥ kham mano buddhir eva cha
ahankāra itīyam me bhinnā prakṛitir aṣhṭadhā

Earth, water, fire, air, space, mind, intellect, and ego—these are eight components of My material energy.

The material energy that comprises this world is amazingly complex and fathomless. By classifying and categorizing it, we make it slightly comprehensible to our finite intellects. The system of classification used in modern science looks on matter as the combination of 118 elements as categorized in the Periodic Table. In the Vedic philosophy and Bhagavad Gita, matter is seen as prakriti, or an energy of God, and eight divisions of this energy are mentioned in this verse.

What Shree Krishna presented to Arjun 5,000 years ago, long before the development of modern science, is the perfect Unified Field Theory. He says, 'Arjun, all that exists in the universe is a manifestation of My material energy.' It is just one material energy that has unfolded into myriad shapes, forms, and entities in this world.

अपरेयमितस्त्वन्यां प्रकृतिं विद्धि मे पराम् ।
जीवभूतां महाबाहो ययेदं धार्यते जगत् ॥ 5 ॥

apareyam itas tvanyām prakṛitim viddhi me parām
jīva-bhūtām mahā-bāho yayedam dhāryate jagat

Such is My inferior energy. But beyond it, O mighty-armed Arjun, I have a superior energy. This is the jiva shakti (the soul energy) which comprises embodied souls who are the basis of life in this world.

Shree Krishna now goes totally beyond the realm of material science to the spiritual. He explains the existence of a superior spiritual energy called *jiva shakti*, which is completely transcendental to insentient matter and encapsulates all souls in this world.

Once we accept the concept of the soul as a form of His energy, then the non-duality of all creation becomes comprehensible. Any energy is simultaneously one and different from the energetic. For example, a fire and its heat and light can be considered as different entities, but they can also be clubbed together and considered as one. Thus, we can consider the soul and God as one from the point of view of the energy (soul) and the Energetic (God). But we can also consider the soul and God as different, since the energy and Energetic are also distinct entities.

The soul is different; matter is different; God is different. Matter is insentient while the soul is sentient, and God is the supremely sentient source and basis of both soul and matter.

एतद्योनीनि भूतानि सर्वाणीत्युपधारय ।
अहं कृत्स्नस्य जगतः प्रभवः प्रलयस्तथा ॥ 6 ॥

etad-yonīni bhūtāni sarvāṇītyupadhāraya
aham kṛitsnasya jagataḥ prabhavaḥ pralayas tathā

Know that all living beings are manifested by these two energies of Mine. I am the source of the entire creation and into Me it again dissolves.

Living beings are a manifestation of God's two energies: jiva shakti, the sentient soul energy, and maya, the insentient material energy or matter. In the material realm, all life is a combination of both matter and soul. Matter by itself is insentient or lifeless, and the sentient soul needs a carrier body. Hence, both come together to form a living being. Similarly, the entire creation is a manifestation of these two energies of God.

मत्तः परतरं नान्यत्किञ्चिदस्ति धनञ्जय ।
मयि सर्वमिदं प्रोतं सूत्रे मणिगणा इव ॥ 7 ॥

mattaḥ parataram nānyat kiñchid asti dhanañjaya
mayi sarvam idam protam sūtre maṇi-gaṇā iva

There is nothing higher than Myself, O Arjun. Everything rests in Me as beads strung on a thread.

The Supreme Lord Shree Krishna now speaks of His paramount position over everything and His dominion over all. He is the Creator, Sustainer, and Annihilator of the universe. He is also the Substratum on which everything exists. The analogy used is of beads strung on a thread. Similarly, although individual souls have free will to act as they wish, it is only granted to them by God, Who upholds them and within whom they exist. Hence, the *Shwetashvatar Upanishad* states:

na tatsamashchābhyadhikashcha dṛishyate parāsya
shaktirvividhaiva shrūyate (6.8)

'There is nothing equal to God, nor is there anything superior to Him.'

दैवी ह्येषा गुणमयी मम माया दुरत्यया ।
मामेव ये प्रपद्यन्ते मायामेतां तरन्ति ते ॥ 14 ॥

daivī hyeṣhā guṇa-mayī mama māyā duratyayā
mām eva ye prapadyante māyām etām taranti te

My divine energy, maya, consisting of the three modes of nature, is very difficult to overcome. But those who surrender unto Me cross over it easily.

Here, Shree Krishna Himself declares that maya is very difficult to overcome because it is His energy. If anyone conquers maya, it means that person has conquered God Himself. Since no one can defeat God, no one can defeat maya either. And because the mind is made from maya, no yogi, jnani, ascetic, or karmi can successfully control the mind merely by self-effort.

The question that comes up now is, 'How can one overcome maya?' Shree Krishna says, 'If you surrender to Me, the Supreme Lord, then by My grace, I will take you across the ocean of material existence. I will indicate to maya that this soul has become Mine. Please leave him.' As an energy of God, maya is subservient to Him. So when it receives this signal from its Master, it immediately releases the soul from bondage.

न मां दुष्कृतिनो मूढाः प्रपद्यन्ते नराधमाः ।
माययापहृतज्ञाना आसुरं भावमाश्रिताः ॥ 15 ॥

na mām duṣhkṛitino mūḍhāḥ prapadyante narādhamāḥ
māyayāpahṛita-jñānā āsuram bhāvam āshritāḥ

Four kinds of people do not surrender unto Me—those ignorant of knowledge, those who lazily follow their lower nature though capable of knowing Me, those with deluded intellect, and those with a demoniac nature.

Shree Krishna lists the four types of people who do not surrender.

1) **The ignorant.** These people are bereft of spiritual knowledge. They are unaware of their identity as the eternal soul and its position as the eternal servant of the Supreme Soul. Thus, their lack of knowledge prevents them from surrendering to God.

2) **Those who lazily follow their lower nature.** These people have basic spiritual knowledge and are aware of what they are supposed to do. However, due to the force of inertia of their lower nature, they do not put in the effort to surrender. This laziness in exerting oneself to act

according to the Vedic principles is a big pitfall on the path of spirituality.

3) **Those with deluded intellect.** These people are very proud of their intellect. Their lack of faith prevents them from accepting the teachings of the Saints and the scriptures. Those who refuse to have faith in anything that is not evident to them in the present, refuse to surrender to God, Who is beyond sense perception. Shree Krishna puts these people in the third category.

4) **Those with a demoniac nature.** These people know there is a God but work in evil and diametrically opposite ways to thwart His purpose in the world. Because of a demoniac nature, they hate God. And as a result, they are repelled by anyone singing His glories or engaging in His devotion. Quite obviously, such people do not surrender to God.

चतुर्विधा भजन्ते मां जनाः सुकृतिनोऽर्जुन ।
आर्तो जिज्ञासुरर्थार्थी ज्ञानी च भरतर्षभ ॥ 16 ॥

तेषां ज्ञानी नित्ययुक्त एकभक्तिर्विशिष्यते ।
प्रियो हि ज्ञानिनोऽत्यर्थमहं स च मम प्रियः ॥ 17 ॥

chatur-vidhā bhajante mām janāḥ sukṛitino 'rjuna
ārto jijñāsur arthārthī jñānī cha bharatarṣhabha

teṣhām jñānī nitya-yukta eka-bhaktir vishiṣhyate
priyo hi jñānino 'tyartham aham sa cha mama priyaḥ

O best amongst the Bharatas, four kinds of pious people engage in My devotion—the distressed, the seekers of

knowledge, the seekers of worldly possessions, and those who are situated in knowledge. Amongst these, I consider them to be the highest, who worship Me with knowledge, and are steadfastly and exclusively devoted to Me. I am very dear to them and they are very dear to Me.

Shree Krishna now categorizes the kinds of people who do take refuge in Him.

1) **The distressed.** For some people, when worldly miseries can no longer be tolerated, it leads them to conclude that running after the world is futile, and it is better to take shelter in God. Likewise, when they see that worldly supports are unable to protect them, they turn to God for protection.

2) **The seekers of knowledge.** Some people take shelter of God out of their curiosity to know. They hear about others finding beatitude in the spiritual realm and this makes them curious to know about the secret behind it. So, to satisfy their curiosity, they approach the Lord.

3) **The seekers of worldly possessions.** Another kind of people are very clear about what they want and are convinced that only the Lord can provide it to them, so they go to His shelter.

4) **Those who are situated in knowledge.** Finally, there are souls who have reached the understanding that they are tiny parts of God and their eternal dharma is to love and serve Him. Shree Krishna says that these are the fourth kind of people who engage in His devotion.

Those who approach God in distress, for worldly possessions, or out of curiosity, do not possess selfless devotion as yet. Slowly, by the process of devotion, their heart becomes pure, and they develop knowledge of their eternal relationship with God. Then their devotion becomes exclusive, selfless, and continuous.

Since they have gained the knowledge that the world does not belong to them and is not a source of happiness, they neither thirst for favourable circumstances nor lament over unfavourable circumstances. They now become situated in selfless devotion. In a spirit of total self-surrender, they offer themselves as oblation in the fire of love for their Divine Beloved. Hence, Shree Krishna says that such devotees who are situated in knowledge are the dearest to Him.

बहूनां जन्मनामन्ते ज्ञानवान्मां प्रपद्यते ।
वासुदेवः सर्वमिति स महात्मा सुदुर्लभः ॥ 19 ॥

bahūnām janmanām ante jñānavān mām prapadyate
vāsudevaḥ sarvam iti sa mahātmā su-durlabhaḥ

After many births of spiritual practice, one who is endowed with knowledge surrenders unto Me, knowing Me to be all that is. Such a great soul is indeed very rare.

True knowledge naturally leads to devotion. The Ramayan states:

jāneṅ binu na hoi paratītī, binu paratīti hoi nahiṅ prītī

'Without knowledge, there cannot be faith; without faith, love cannot grow.' Thus, true knowledge is naturally accompanied by love. If we claim we possess knowledge of Brahman, but feel no love towards Him, then our knowledge is merely theoretical.

Here, Shree Krishna explains that after many lifetimes of cultivation of knowledge, when that jnani's knowledge matures into true wisdom, he surrenders to the Supreme Lord, knowing Him to be all that is. Such a noble soul is very rare. He does not say this for karmis, Ashtang yogis, ascetics, or others. He declares it for the devotee and says that the exalted soul who realizes 'All is God' and surrenders to Him, is very rare.

नाहं प्रकाशः सर्वस्य योगमायासमावृतः ।
मूढोऽयं नाभिजानाति लोको मामजमव्ययम् ॥ 25 ॥

nāham prakāshaḥ sarvasya yoga-māyā-samāvṛitaḥ
mūḍho 'yam nābhijānāti loko mām ajam avyayam

I am not manifest to everyone, being veiled by My divine Yogmaya energy. Hence, those without knowledge do not know that I am without birth and changeless.

Having described two of His energies in verses 7.4 and 7.5, Shree Krishna now mentions a third energy—Yogmaya, His supreme energy. Jagadguru Kripaluji Maharaj states:

shaktimān kī shaktiyāñ, aganita yadapi bakhān
tin mahañ 'māyā', 'jīva', aru 'parā', trishakti pradhān

(*Bhakti Shatak* verse 3)

'The Supreme Energetic Shree Krishna has infinite energies. Among these, Yogmaya (supreme divine energy), the souls (jiva shakti), and maya (insentient material energy) are the main ones.'

The divine power, Yogmaya, is God's all-powerful energy. Through it, He manifests His divine love, divine bliss, and divine abodes. By that Yogmaya power, God descends in the world and manifests His divine pastimes on the earth plane as well. Although God is seated in our hearts, we do not have any perception of His presence within us. Yogmaya keeps His divinity obscured from us until we are eligible for His divine vision. Hence, even if we see the Lord in His personal form, we will not be able to recognize Him as God. It is only when the Yogmaya power bestows its grace upon us that we get the divine vision to see and recognize God as He truly is.

The Yogmaya power is both formless and manifests in the personal form, such as Radha, Sita, Durga, Kali, Lakshmi, and Parvati, and so on. These are all divine forms of the Yogmaya energy, and all are revered in Vedic culture as the Mother of the universe. They radiate the motherly qualities of tenderness, compassion, forgiveness, sacrifice, grace, and causeless love. More importantly for us, They bestow divine grace upon the soul and grant it the transcendental knowledge by which it can know God.

Chapter 8

Akshar Brahma Yog

The Yog of the Eternal God

यं यं वापि स्मरन्भावं त्यजत्यन्ते कलेवरम् ।
तं तमेवैति कौन्तेय सदा तद्भावभावित: ॥ 6 ॥

yam yam vāpi smaran bhāvam tyajatyante kalevaram
tam tam evaiti kaunteya sadā tad-bhāva-bhāvitaḥ

Whatever one remembers upon giving up the body at the time of death, O son of Kunti, one attains that state, being always absorbed in such contemplation.

According to Shree Krishna, whatever prominently dominates one's thoughts at the moment of death will determine one's next birth. One's final thoughts will naturally be determined by what was constantly contemplated and meditated upon during the span of life, as influenced by one's daily habits and associations.

One should not conclude on reading the verse that for the attainment of the ultimate goal, the Supreme Lord is only to be meditated upon at the moment of death. This is impossible without a lifetime of preparation. Death is such a painful experience that the mind naturally gravitates to the thoughts that are a part of one's chitta (subconscious mind). Only if we contemplate something continuously does it manifest as a part of our inner nature. So, to develop a heart full of devotion, the Lord must be remembered, recollected, and contemplated upon at every moment of our life.

तस्मात्सर्वेषु कालेषु मामनुस्मर युध्य च ।
मय्यर्पितमनोबुद्धिर्मामेवैष्यस्यसंशयम् ॥ 7 ॥

tasmāt sarveṣhu kāleṣhu mām anusmara yudhya cha
mayyarpita-mano-buddhir mām evaiṣhyasyasanshayam

Therefore, always remember Me and also do your duty of fighting the war. With mind and intellect surrendered to Me, you will definitely attain Me; of this, there is no doubt.

The first line of this verse is the essence of the teachings of the Bhagavad Gita. It has the power to make our life divine. It also encapsulates the definition of karm yog. Shree Krishna says, 'Keep your mind attached to Me, and do your worldly duty with your body.' This applies to people in all walks of life—doctors, engineers, lawyers, housewives, students, and everyone else.

Some people neglect their worldly duties on the plea that they have taken to spirituality. Others excuse themselves from spiritual practice on the pretext of worldly engagements. People believe that spiritual and material pursuits are irreconcilable. But God's message is to sanctify one's entire life.

When we practise such karm yog, worldly works will not suffer because the body is actively engaged in them. But since the mind is attached to God, these actions will not bind one in the Law of Karma. Only those activities result in karmic reactions which are performed with attachment.

The condition for karm yog has been stated very clearly in this verse: The mind must be constantly engaged in thinking of God. The moment the mind forgets God, it comes under the attack of the big generals of maya's army—lust, anger, greed, envy, hatred, and other negative emotions. Consequently, it is important to always keep it attached to God.

Often people claim to be karm yogis because they say they do both—karm and yog. For the major part of the day, they do karm, and for a few minutes, they do yog (meditation on God). But this is not the definition of karm yog that Shree Krishna has given. He states: 1) even while doing work, the mind must be engaged in thinking of God, and 2) the remembrance of God must not be intermittent but constant throughout the day.

अनन्यचेताः सततं यो मां स्मरति नित्यशः ।
तस्याहं सुलभः पार्थ नित्ययुक्तस्य योगिनः ॥ 14 ॥

ananya-chetāḥ satatam yo mām smarati nityashaḥ
tasyāham sulabhaḥ pārtha nitya-yuktasya yoginaḥ

O Parth, for those yogis who always think of Me with exclusive devotion, I am easily attainable because of their constant absorption in Me.

In the entire Bhagavad Gita, this is the only verse in which Shree Krishna says that He is easy to attain. However, the condition He states is *ananya-chetāḥ* which means that the mind must be exclusively absorbed in Him and Him alone. The word *ananya* is very important. Etymologically, it means *na anya* or 'no other'. The mind should be attached to no one else but God alone. This condition of exclusivity has often been repeated in the Bhagavad Gita.

ananyāsh chintayanto mām (9.22)

tam eva sharaṇam gachchha (18.62)

mām ekam sharaṇam vraja (18.66)

Exclusive devotion means that the mind must be attached only to the names, forms, virtues, pastimes, abodes, and associates of God. The logic is very simple. The aim of sadhana is to purify the mind, and this is accomplished only by attaching it to the all-pure God. However, if we cleanse the mind by contemplating upon God and then again dirty it by dipping it in worldliness, then no matter how long we try, we will never be able to clean it.

This is exactly the mistake that many people make. They love God, but they also love and get attached to worldly people and objects. So whatever positive gains they accomplish through sadhana become tarnished by worldly attachment. If you apply soap on a cloth to clean it, but simultaneously keep throwing dirt upon it, your effort will be an exercise in futility. Hence, Shree Krishna says that it is not just devotion but exclusive devotion to Him that makes Him easily attainable.

Chapter 9

Raja Vidya Yog

Yog through the King of Sciences

राजविद्या राजगुह्यं पवित्रमिदमुत्तमम् ।
प्रत्यक्षावगमं धर्म्यं सुसुखं कर्तुमव्ययम् ॥ 2 ॥

rāja-vidyā rāja-guhyam pavitram idam uttamam
pratyakṣhāvagamam dharmyam su-sukham kartum avyayam

This knowledge is the king of sciences and the most profound of all secrets. It purifies those who hear it. It is directly realizable, in accordance with dharma, easy to practise, and everlasting in effect.

Raja means 'king'. Shree Krishna uses the metaphor 'raja' to emphasize the paramount position of the knowledge He is going to reveal.

Vidyā means 'science'. He does not refer to His teachings as creed, religion, dogma, doctrine, or belief. He declares that what He is going to describe to Arjun is the 'king of sciences'.

Guhya means 'secret'. This knowledge is also the supreme secret.

In the second chapter, Shree Krishna explained the knowledge of the atma (soul) as a separate and distinct entity from the body. This is *guhya*, or secret knowledge. In the seventh and eighth chapters, He explained knowledge of His powers, which is *guhyatar*, or more secret. And in the ninth and subsequent chapters, He will reveal knowledge of His pure bhakti, which is *guhyatam*, or the most secret.

Pavitram means 'pure'. Knowledge of devotion is supremely pure because it is untainted by petty selfishness. It inspires sacrifice of the self at the altar of divine love for the Supreme Lord.

Pratyakṣha means 'directly perceptible'. The practice of the science of bhakti begins with a leap of faith and results in direct perception of God. It is not unlike the methodology of other sciences, where we begin an experiment with a hypothesis and conclude with a verified result.

Dharmyam means 'virtuous'. Devotion performed without desire for material rewards is the most virtuous action. It is continuously nourished by righteous acts, such as service to the Guru.

Kartum susukham means 'very easy to practise'. God does not need anything from us; He is attained very naturally if we love Him selflessly.

When this is the sovereign science and easy to practise, then why do people not apply themselves to learning it? Shree Krishna explains this next.

अश्रद्दधानाः पुरुषा धर्मस्यास्य परन्तप ।
अप्राप्य मां निवर्तन्ते मृत्युसंसारवर्त्मनि ॥ 3 ॥

ashraddadhānāḥ purușhā dharmasyāsya parantapa
aprāpya mām nivartante mṛityu-samsāra-vartmani

People who have no faith in this dharma are unable to attain Me, O conqueror of enemies. They repeatedly come back to this world in the cycle of birth and death.

In this verse, Shree Krishna calls knowledge of loving devotion to God 'dharma', implying all should follow this path. Yet, no matter how wonderful the knowledge and how effective the path, it remains useless for one who refuses to walk on it.

Often people say that they are only willing to believe in what they can directly perceive, and since there is no immediate perception of God, they do not believe in Him. However, the fact is that we believe in so many things in the world too, without direct perception of them. A judge delivers judgement on a case concerning an event that took place many years in the past. If the judge adopted the philosophy of believing only what he or she had directly experienced, then the entire legal system would fail. So, even in material activities, faith is required at every step.

Belief in God is not a natural process that we as human beings just follow. We have to exercise our free will and actively make a decision to have faith in God. The Supreme Lord says that those who choose not to have faith in the spiritual path remain bereft of divine wisdom and continue to rotate in the cycle of life and death.

महात्मानस्तु मां पार्थ दैवीं प्रकृतिमाश्रिताः ।
भजन्त्यनन्यमनसो ज्ञात्वा भूतादिमव्ययम् ॥ 13 ॥

mahātmānas tu mām pārtha daivīm prakṛitim āshritāḥ
bhajantyananya-manaso jñātvā bhūtādim avyayam

But the great souls, who take shelter of My divine energy, O Parth, know Me, Lord Krishna, as the Origin of all creation. They engage in My devotion with their mind fixed exclusively on Me.

For souls who are sleeping under the sway of maya, material life is a prolonged dream. In contrast, great souls are those who have woken up from their ignorance and brushed aside material consciousness like a bad dream. Released from the grips of maya, they are now under the shelter of the Yogmaya energy. Such enlightened souls accept the spiritual reality of their eternal relationship with God.

Just as God has both aspects to His personality—the formless and the personal form—His Yogmaya energy also possesses both aspects. It is a formless energy, but it also manifests in the personal form as Radha, Sita, Durga, Lakshmi, Kali, and Parvati. They are non-different from each other, just as Krishna, Ram, Shiv, and Narayan are non-different forms of the one God.

In this verse, Shree Krishna mentions that great souls take shelter of Yogmaya. The reason is that divine grace, knowledge, and love, all are God's energies and subservient to Yogmaya energy, which is Radha. Hence, by the grace of Yogmaya, one receives the love, knowledge, and grace of God. Great souls, who receive divine grace, become endowed with divine love and engage in uninterrupted devotion to God.

सततं कीर्तयन्तो मां यतन्तश्च दृढव्रताः ।
नमस्यन्तश्च मां भक्त्या नित्ययुक्ता उपासते ॥ 14 ॥

satatam kīrtayanto mām yatantash cha dṛiḍha-vratāḥ
namasyantash cha mām bhaktyā nitya-yuktā upāsate

Always singing My divine glories, striving with great determination, and humbly bowing down before Me, they constantly worship Me in loving devotion.

Having said that the great souls engage in His devotion, Shree Krishna now explains how they do bhakti. He says that devotees become attached to kirtan as a means of practising their devotion and enhancing it. Chanting of the glories of the Lord is called kirtan which is defined as: *nāma-līlā-guṇadīnām uchchair-bhāṣhā tu kīrtanam* (*Bhakti Rasamrit Sindhu* 1.2.145) 'Singing glories of the names, forms, qualities, pastimes, abodes, and associates of God is called kirtan.'

Kirtan is one of the most powerful means of practising bhakti. It involves the three-fold devotion of *shravan* (hearing), *kirtan* (chanting), and *smaran* (remembering). The goal is to fix the mind upon God, which becomes easier when done together with hearing and chanting.

Kirtan has many other benefits as well. Often when people practise devotion through japa (chanting of mantra or name of God on rosary beads) or plain meditation, they find themselves overwhelmed by sleep. However, kirtan is such an engaging process that it usually drives sleep away. Also, chanting blocks out distracting sounds from the environment. Kirtan can be practised in groups which enables mass participation. In addition, the mind desires variety which it gets through the medium of kirtan in the form of the names, virtues, pastimes, abodes, etc., of God. And since kirtan involves loud chanting, the divine vibrations of the names of God make the entire environment auspicious and holy.

The Vedic scriptures particularly extol kirtan as the simplest and most powerful process of devotion in the present age of Kali.

kṛite yad dhyāyato viṣhṇum tretāyām yajato makhaiḥ
dwāpare paricharyāyām kalau tad dhari-kīrtanāt

(Bhagavatam 12.3.52)

'The best process of devotion in the age of *Satya* was simple meditation upon God. In the age of *Tretā*, it was the performance of sacrifices for the pleasure of God. In the age of *Dwāpar*, worship of the deities was the recommended process. In the present age of *Kali*, it is kirtan alone.'

However, one must remember that in the process of kirtan, hearing and chanting are supports. The essence is to remember God. If we leave it out, kirtan will not purify the mind. Thus, Shree Krishna says that His devotees do kirtan while constantly engaging the mind in thoughts of Him. They practise this with great determination for the purification of the mind.

अनन्याश्चिन्तयन्तो मां ये जनाः पर्युपासते ।
तेषां नित्याभियुक्तानां योगक्षेमं वहाम्यहम् ॥ 22 ॥

ananyāsh chintayanto mām ye janāḥ paryupāsate
teṣhām nityābhiyuktānām yoga-kṣhemam vahāmyaham

There are those who always think of Me and engage in exclusive devotion to Me. To them, whose mind is always absorbed in Me, I provide what they lack and preserve what they already possess.

A mother never thinks of deserting her helpless newborn child who is entirely dependent upon her. The supreme and eternal mother of the soul is God. In this verse, God offers motherly assurance to souls who surrender exclusively to Him. The words used are *vahāmi aham*, meaning 'I personally carry the burden of maintaining My devotees', just as a married man carries the responsibility of maintaining his wife and children.

So, in this verse, God promises two things. The first is *yog*—He bestows His devotees the spiritual assets they do not possess. The second is *kṣhem*—He protects the spiritual assets that His devotees already possess. However, the condition He places for this is exclusive surrender.

पत्रं पुष्पं फलं तोयं यो मे भक्त्या प्रयच्छति ।
तदहं भक्त्युपहृतमश्नामि प्रयतात्मनः ॥ 26 ॥

patram puṣhpam phalam toyam yo me bhaktyā prayachchhati
tadaham bhaktyupahṛitam ashnāmi prayatātmanaḥ

If one offers to Me with devotion a leaf, a flower, a fruit, or even water, I delightfully partake of that item offered with love by My devotee in pure consciousness.

Shree Krishna now explains the ease of engaging in devotion to the Supreme. In the worship of the devatas and the ancestors, there are many rules to propitiate them, all of which must be strictly followed. But God accepts anything that is offered with a loving heart. If you only have fruit, offer it to God, and He will be pleased. If fruit is unavailable, offer Him a flower. If it is not the season for flowers, offer God a mere leaf; even that will suffice, provided it is a gift of love. If leaves are also scarce during autumn and winter, offer water, which is available everywhere. The important point is to make all offerings with love. The word *bhaktyā* has been used in both the first and second lines of the verse to convey that it is the bhakti of the devotee that is pleasing to God and not the value of the offering.

यत्करोषि यदश्नासि यज्जुहोषि ददासि यत् ।
यत्तपस्यसि कौन्तेय तत्कुरुष्व मदर्पणम् ॥ 27 ॥

yat karoṣhi yad ashnāsi yaj juhoṣhi dadāsi yat
yat tapasyasi kaunteya tat kuruṣhva mad-arpaṇam

Whatever you do, whatever you eat, whatever you offer as oblation to the sacred fire, whatever you bestow as a gift, and whatever austerities you perform, O son of Kunti, do them as an offering to Me.

In the previous verse, Shree Krishna stated that all objects should be offered to Him. Now He says that all actions should also be offered to Him. Whatever social duties one may be engaged in, whatever vegetarian food one may be eating, whatever non-alcoholic beverages one may be drinking, whatever Vedic rites one may perform, whatever vows and austerities one may observe, all should be offered mentally to the Supreme Lord. Very often, people separate devotion from their daily life and look on it as something that is only to be performed inside the temple room. However, devotion is not to be restricted to the periphery of the temple walls; it is to be engaged in at every moment of our life.

समोऽहं सर्वभूतेषु न मे द्वेष्योऽस्ति न प्रियः ।
ये भजन्ति तु मां भक्त्या मयि ते तेषु चाप्यहम् ॥ 29 ॥

samo 'ham sarva-bhūteṣhu na me dveṣhyo 'sti na priyaḥ
ye bhajanti tu mām bhaktyā mayi te teṣhu chāpyaham

I am equally disposed to all living beings; I am neither inimical nor partial to anyone. But the devotees who worship Me with love reside in Me and I reside in them.

We all intuitively believe that if there is a God, He must be perfectly just; there cannot be an unjust God.

However, in this verse Shree Krishna creates the doubt that God is partial towards His devotees, because while everyone is subject to the Law of Karma, God releases His devotees from it. Isn't this symptomatic of the flaw of partiality? Shree Krishna feels it necessary to clarify this point and begins the verse by saying *samo 'ham* , meaning 'No, no, I am equal to all. But I have a uniform law in accordance with which I bestow My grace.' The law He is referring to secretly is the Law of Surrender which was previously stated in verse 4.11: 'In whatever way people surrender unto Me, I reciprocate accordingly.'

Rainwater falls equally upon the earth. Yet, the drop that falls on the cornfields gets converted into grain; the drop that falls on the desert bush gets converted into a thorn; the drop that falls in the gutter becomes dirty water; and the drop that falls in the oyster becomes a pearl. There is no partiality on the part of the rain since it is equitable in bestowing its grace upon the land. The raindrops cannot be held responsible for this variation in results which are a consequence of the nature of the recipient. Similarly, God states here that He is equally disposed towards all living beings, and yet, those who do not love Him are bereft of the benefits of His grace because their hearts are unsuitable vessels for receiving it.

मन्मना भव मद्भक्तो मद्याजी मां नमस्कुरु ।
मामेवैष्यसि युक्त्वैवमात्मानं मत्परायणः ॥ 34 ॥

man-manā bhava mad-bhakto mad-yājī mām namaskuru
mām evaiṣhyasi yuktvaivam ātmānam mat-parāyaṇaḥ

Always think of Me, be devoted to Me, worship Me, and offer obeisance to Me. Having dedicated your mind and body to Me, you will certainly come to Me.

Having stressed bhakti, the path of devotion, throughout this chapter, Shree Krishna now concludes it by entreating Arjun to become His devotee. He asks Arjun to unite his consciousness with God in true yog, by worshipping Him, engaging the mind in meditation upon His divine form, and offering obeisance in pure humility to Him.

Namaskuru (the act of humble obeisance) effectively neutralizes vestiges of egotism that may arise in the performance of devotion. Thus, free from pride, with the heart immersed in devotion, one should dedicate all one's thoughts and actions to the Supreme just as all rivers flow into the ocean. Shree Krishna assures Arjun that such complete communion with Him through bhakti yog will definitely result in the attainment of God-realization; of this, there should be no doubt.

Chapter 10

Vibhuti Yog

Yog through Appreciating the Infinite Opulences of God

बुद्धिर्ज्ञानमसम्मोहः क्षमा सत्यं दमः शमः ।
सुखं दुःखं भवोऽभावो भयं चाभयमेव च ॥ 4 ॥

अहिंसा समता तुष्टिस्तपो दानं यशोऽयशः ।
भवन्ति भावा भूतानां मत्त एव पृथग्विधाः ॥ 5 ॥

buddhir jñānam asammohaḥ kṣhamā satyam damaḥ shamaḥ
sukham duḥkham bhavo 'bhāvo bhayam chābhayameva cha

ahinsā samatā tuṣhṭis tapo dānam yaśho 'yashaḥ
bhavanti bhāvā bhūtānām matta eva pṛithag-vidhāḥ

From Me alone arise the varieties of qualities in humans, such as intellect, knowledge, clarity of thought, forgiveness, truthfulness, control over the senses and mind, joy and sorrow, birth and death, fear and courage, non-violence, equanimity, contentment, austerity, charity, fame, and infamy.

In these two verses, Lord Krishna continues to confirm his Supreme Lordship and absolute dominion over all that exists in creation. Here, He mentions 20 emotions that manifest in a variety of degrees and combinations in different people to form the individual fabric of human nature. He declares that the various moods, temperaments, and dispositions of humans emanate from Him alone.

Hence, He is the source of all good and bad natures in living beings.

This can be compared to the power supplied by the electrical station that is used by various gadgets at home. The same electric power that passes through different gadgets creates different effects. It generates sound in one, light in the other, and heat in the third. Although the manifestations are different, their source is the same—the electrical station. Similarly, the energy of God manifests in us positively or negatively according to our *puruṣhārth* (the actions we perform by exercising our freedom of choice) in the present and past lives.

अहं सर्वस्य प्रभवो मत्तः सर्वं प्रवर्तते ।
इति मत्वा भजन्ते मां बुधा भावसमन्विताः ॥ 8 ॥

aham sarvasya prabhavo mattaḥ sarvam pravartate
iti matvā bhajante mām budhā bhāva-samanvitāḥ

I am the Origin of all creation. Everything proceeds from Me. The wise who know this perfectly worship Me with great faith and devotion.

Shree Krishna begins the verse by saying *aham sarvasya prabhavo*, meaning 'I am the Supreme Ultimate Truth and the Cause of all causes'. The wise who comprehend this truth develop firm faith and worship Him with loving devotion.

मच्चित्ता मद्गतप्राणा बोधयन्तः परस्परम् ।
कथयन्तश्च मां नित्यं तुष्यन्ति च रमन्ति च ॥ 9 ॥

mach-chittā mad-gata-prāṇā bodhayantaḥ parasparam
kathayantash cha mām nityam tuṣhyanti cha ramanti cha

With their mind fixed on Me and their life surrendered to Me, My devotees remain ever content in Me. They derive great satisfaction and bliss in enlightening one another about Me and in conversing about My glories.

The nature of the mind is to become absorbed in what it likes most. Devotees of the Lord become absorbed in remembering Him because they develop deep adoration for Him. His devotion becomes the basis of their life, from which they derive meaning, purpose, and the strength to live. They feel it as essential to remember God as a fish feels the need to be surrounded by water.

What is most dear to people's hearts can be determined by where they dedicate their mind, body, and wealth. Likewise, the love of the devotees manifests in the dedication of their every word, thought, and deed to God. Shree Krishna says: *mad-gata-prāṇāḥ*, implying 'My devotees surrender their life to Me.'

From such surrender, comes contentment. Since devotees offer the results of their activities to their Beloved Lord, they see every situation as coming from Him. Hence, they gladly accept both positive and negative circumstances as the will of God and remain equipoised in both.

While the devotees' love for God is displayed in the above sentiments, it also manifests on their lips. They find great relish in conversing about the glories of God, and in His names, forms, virtues, pastimes, abodes, and associates.

In this way, by engaging in *kirtan* (chanting) and *shravan* (hearing) about the glories of God, they savour His sweetness and share it with others as well. They contribute to one another's progress by enlightening others about divine knowledge of God (*bodhayanti*). Speaking and singing about the glories of God gives the devotees great satisfaction (*tuṣhyanti*) and delight (*ramanti*). In this way, they worship Him through the processes of remembering, hearing, and chanting. This is the three-fold bhakti comprising *shravan, kirtan*, and *smaran.*

तेषां सततयुक्तानां भजतां प्रीतिपूर्वकम् ।
ददामि बुद्धियोगं तं येन मामुपयान्ति ते ॥ 10 ॥

teṣhām satata-yuktānām bhajatām prīti-pūrvakam
dadāmi buddhi-yogam tam yena mām upayānti te

To those whose mind is always united with Me in loving devotion, I give the divine knowledge by which they can attain Me.

Divine knowledge of God is not attained by the flight of our intellect because it is made from maya. So, it follows that our thoughts, understanding, and wisdom are confined to the material realm; God and His divine realm remain entirely beyond the scope of our corporeal intellect. The Vedas emphatically declare: 'Those who think they can understand God with their intellect have no understanding of God. Only those who think that He is beyond the scope of their comprehension truly understand Him' (*Kenopanishad* 2.3).

If we cannot know God, then how can we love and attain Him? Shree Krishna reveals that it is God who bestows divine knowledge upon the soul, and the fortunate soul who receives His grace is able to know Him. Thus, true knowledge of God is not a result of intellectual gymnastics but a consequence of divine grace. Shree Krishna also mentions in this verse that He does not choose the recipients of His grace in a whimsical manner. Rather, he bestows it on those who unite their mind with Him in devotion.

यद्यद्विभूतिमत्सत्त्वं श्रीमदूर्जितमेव वा ।
तत्तदेवावगच्छ त्वं मम तेजोंऽशसम्भवम् ॥ 41 ॥

yad yad vibhūtimat sattvam shrīmad ūrjitam eva vā
tat tad evāvagachchha tvam mama tejo 'nsha-sambhavam

Whatever you see as beautiful, glorious, or powerful, know it to spring from but a spark of My splendour.

While God's opulences are unlimited, in verses 20–39, Shree Krishna reveals 82 of them in response to Arjun's quest to know more about God. A sample of these is listed below.

I am seated in the heart of all living entities. I am the beginning, middle, and end of all beings. (10.20)

Among luminous objects, I am the sun...and the moon among the stars in the night sky. (10.21)

I am the *Sama Veda* amongst the Vedas... Amongst the senses, I am the mind; amongst the living beings, I am consciousness. (10.22)

Amongst the rudras, know Me to be Shankar... I am Agni amongst the vasus. (10.23)

I am...the transcendental Om amongst sounds. Amongst chants, know Me to be the Holy Name; amongst the immovable things, I am the Himalayas. (10.25)

Amongst trees, I am the peepal tree; of the celestial sages, I am Narad. (10.26)

Amongst the snakes, I am Anant (Shesh)...amongst dispensers of law, I am Yamraj, the lord of death. (10.29)

Amongst purifiers, I am the wind, amongst wielders of weapons, I am Ram...of flowing rivers, I am the Ganges. (10.31)

Know Me to be the beginning, middle, and end of all creation. Amongst sciences, I am the science of spirituality, and in debates, I am the logical conclusion. (10.32)

I am the beginning 'A' amongst all letters. I am the endless Time, and amongst creators, I am Brahma. (10.33)

I am the all-devouring death, and I am the origin of those things that are yet to be. Amongst feminine qualities, I am fame, prosperity, fine speech, memory, intelligence, courage, and forgiveness. (10.34)

I am the gambling of the cheats and the splendour of the splendid. I am the victory of the victorious, the resolve of the resolute, and the virtue of the virtuous. (10.36)

Amongst the descendants of Vrishni, I am Krishna, and amongst the Pandavas I am Arjun. Know me to be Ved

Vyas amongst the sages, and Shukracharya amongst the great thinkers. (10.37)

I am just punishment amongst means of preventing lawlessness, and proper conduct amongst those who seek victory. Amongst secrets I am silence, and in the wise I am their wisdom. (10.38)

I am the generating seed of all living beings, O Arjun. No creature moving or non-moving can exist without Me. (10.39)

The mind is naturally drawn to specialties, and thus, the Lord has revealed these outstanding features among His powers. Whenever we see a special splendour manifesting anywhere, if we look on it as God's glory, then our mind will naturally be transported to Him. In the larger scheme of things, however, since God's glories are in all things big and small, one can think of the whole world as providing innumerable examples for us to enhance our devotion. A paint company in India would advertise, 'Whenever you see colours, think of us.' In this case, Shree Krishna's statement is tantamount to saying, 'Wherever you see a manifestation of glory, think of Me.'

अथवा बहुनैतेन किं ज्ञातेन तवार्जुन ।
विष्टभ्याहमिदं कृत्स्नमेकांशेन स्थितो जगत् ॥ 42 ॥

atha vā bahunaitena kim jñātena tavārjuna
viṣhṭabhyāham idam kṛitsnam ekānshena sthito jagat

What need is there for all this detailed knowledge,

O Arjun? Simply know that by one fraction of My being, I pervade and support this entire creation.

Having revealed many amazing aspects of His splendour, Shree Krishna says that the magnitude of His glory cannot be judged even from the sum total of what He has described, for the entire creation of unlimited universes is held within a fraction of His Being.

Why does He make a reference to a fraction of His Being? The reason is that the entire material creation consisting of unlimited universes is only one-fourth of God's entire manifestation; the remaining three-fourths is His spiritual creation.

pādo 'sya vishwā bhūtāni, tripādasyāmṛitam divi

(*Purush Sūktam*, mantra 3)

'This temporary world made from material energy is but one part of the Supreme Divine Personality. The other three parts are His eternal abodes that are beyond the phenomenon of life and death.'

Interestingly, at Kurukshetra, in this material realm, Shree Krishna is standing in front of Arjun, yet He reveals that the entire world is within a fraction of His Being.

Chapter 11

Vishwaroop Darshan Yog

Yog through Beholding the Cosmic Form of God

एवमेतद्यथात्थ त्वमात्मानं परमेश्वर ।
द्रष्टुमिच्छामि ते रूपमैश्वरं पुरुषोत्तम ॥ 3 ॥

evam etad yathāttha tvam ātmānam parameshvara
draṣhṭum ichchhāmi te rūpam aishwaram puruṣhottama

O Supreme Lord, You are precisely what You declare Yourself to be. Now I desire to see Your divine cosmic form, O Greatest of persons.

Arjun declares that he accepts the reality of Shree Krishna's divine personality, precisely as has been described to him. He has complete faith in His personal form, and yet, he desires to see Shree Krishna's vishwarup, or universal form, replete with all opulences. He wishes to view it with his own eyes.

न तु मां शक्यसे द्रष्टुमनेनैव स्वचक्षुषा ।
दिव्यं ददामि ते चक्षुः पश्य मे योगमैश्वरम् ॥ 8 ॥

na tu mām shakyase draṣhṭum anenaiva sva-chakṣhuṣhā
divyam dadāmi te chakṣhuḥ pashya me yogam aishwaram

But you cannot see My cosmic form with these physical eyes of yours. Therefore, I grant you divine vision. Behold My majestic opulence!

When the Supreme Lord descends in the world, He has two kinds of forms—one is the material form that can be seen with material eyes, and the other is His divine form that can only be seen with divine vision. Thus, during His descension upon the earth, we see only His material form; His divine form is not visible to our material eyes.

So now, Shree Krishna says that He will grant the divine vision with which it will become possible to behold the universal form with all its majesty.

The next few verses describe the wonder of the glorious form.

In that cosmic form, Arjun saw unlimited faces and eyes, decorated with many celestial ornaments and wielding many kinds of divine weapons. He wore many garlands on His body and was anointed with many sweet-smelling heavenly fragrances. He revealed Himself as the wonderful and infinite Lord whose face is everywhere. (11.10–11)

If a thousand suns were to blaze forth together in the sky, they would not match the splendour of that great form. (11.12)

There Arjun could see the totality of the entire universe established in one place, in that body of the God of gods. (11.13)

Arjun is not just amazed and awestruck but fearful of this form. He says:

O mighty Lord, in veneration of Your magnificent form with its many mouths, eyes, arms, thighs, legs, stomachs, and terrifying teeth, all the worlds are terror-stricken, and so am I. (11.23)

O Lord Vishnu, seeing Your form touching the sky, effulgent in many colours, with mouths wide open and enormous blazing eyes, my heart is trembling with fear. I have lost all courage and peace of mind. (11.24)

Having seen Your many mouths bearing Your terrible teeth, resembling the raging fire at the time of annihilation, I forget where I am and do not know where to go. O Lord of lords, You are the shelter of the universe; please have mercy on me. (11.25)

Tell me who You are, so fierce of form. O God of gods, I bow before You; please bestow Your mercy on me. You, who existed before all creation, I wish to know who You are, for I do not comprehend Your nature and workings. (11.31)

Finally, he pleads to the Lord to return to His loving two-armed form that Arjun is so comfortable and familiar with. He prays: 'Having seen Your universal form that I had never seen before, I feel great joy. And yet, my mind trembles with fear. Please have mercy on me and again show me Your pleasing form, O God of gods, O Abode of the universe.'

श्रीभगवानुवाच ।
सुदुर्दर्शमिदं रूपं दृष्टवानसि यन्मम ।
देवा अप्यस्य रूपस्य नित्यं दर्शनकाङ्‍क्षिणः ॥ 52 ॥

नाहं वेदैर्न तपसा न दानेन न चेज्यया ।
शक्य एवंविधो द्रष्टुं दृष्टवानसि मां यथा ॥ 53 ॥

shrī-bhagavān uvācha
su-durdarsham idam rūpam dṛiṣhṭavān asi yan mama
devā apy asya rūpasya nityam darshana-kāṅkṣhiṇaḥ

nāham vedair na tapasā na dānena na chejyayā
shakya evam-vidho draṣhṭum dṛiṣhṭavān asi mām yathā

The Supreme Lord said: This form of Mine that you are seeing is exceedingly difficult to behold. Even the celestial gods are eager to see it. Neither by the study of the Vedas, nor by penance, charity, or fire sacrifices, can I be seen as you have seen Me.

भक्त्या त्वनन्यया शक्य अहमेवंविधोऽर्जुन ।
ज्ञातुं द्रष्टुं च तत्त्वेन प्रवेष्टुं च परन्तप ॥ 54 ॥

bhaktyā tv ananyayā shakya aham evam-vidho 'rjuna
jñātum draṣhṭum cha tattvena praveṣhṭum cha parantapa

O Arjun, by unalloyed devotion alone can I be known as I am, standing before you. Thereby, on receiving My divine vision, O scorcher of foes, one can enter into union with Me.

After showing Arjun His awe-inspiring cosmic form, at Arjun's request, Shree Krishna returns to His two-armed form. This is the form that is most easily relatable to us. So again, Shree Krishna emphasizes bhakti as the superior path to attain the loving two-armed form.

मत्कर्मकृन्मत्परमो मद्भक्तः सङ्गवर्जितः ।
निर्वैरः सर्वभूतेषु यः स मामेति पाण्डव ॥ 55 ॥

mat-karma-kṛin mat-paramo mad-bhaktaḥ saṅga-varjitaḥ
nirvairaḥ sarva-bhūteṣhu yaḥ sa mām eti pāṇḍava

Those who perform all their duties for My sake, who depend upon Me and are devoted to Me, who are free from attachment and are without malice towards all beings, such devotees certainly come to Me.

Shree Krishna now concludes this chapter by highlighting five characteristics of those who engage in exclusive devotion and the result of such single-minded devotion.

They perform all their duties for My sake. Accomplished devotees do not divide their works into material and spiritual. They perform every work for the pleasure of God, thus consecrating every act of theirs to Him. Saint Kabir states:

jahañ jahañ chalūñ karūñ parikramā, jo jo karūñ so sevā
jaba sovūñ karūñ daṇḍavat, jānūñ deva na dūjā

'When I walk, I think I am circumambulating the Lord; when I work, I think I am serving the Lord; and when I sleep, I think I am offering Him obeisance. In this manner, I perform no activity other than that which is offered to Him.'

They depend upon Me. Those who rely upon their spiritual practices to reach God are not exclusively dependent upon Him. That is because He is attained by His grace and not by spiritual practice. His exclusive devotees do not even rely upon their devotion as a means of attaining Him. Rather, they place their entire faith in His grace alone and see their devotion as merely a way of attracting divine grace.

They are devoted to Me. The devotees do not feel the need for performing any other spiritual practices, such as cultivation of the knowledge of *Sankhya,* practice of ashtang yog, performance of fire sacrifices, etc. In this way, they feel that their relationship is with God alone. They behold only their Beloved Lord pervading all objects and personalities.

They are free from attachment. Devotion requires the engagement of the mind. This is only possible if the mind is detached from the world. So exclusive devotees are free from all worldly attachments and repose their mind in God alone.

They are without malice towards all beings. If the heart fills up with malice, it will again not remain exclusive towards God. Thus, exclusive devotees do not harbour any malice, even towards those who have harmed them. Instead, thinking that God resides in the heart of all beings, they see all actions as stemming from Him, and so they forgive even their wrongdoers.

Chapter 12

Bhakti Yog

The Yog of Devotion

अर्जुन उवाच ।
एवं सततयुक्ता ये भक्तास्त्वां पर्युपासते ।
ये चाप्यक्षरमव्यक्तं तेषां के योगवित्तमाः ॥ 1 ॥

arjuna uvācha
evam satata-yuktā ye bhaktās tvām paryupāsate
ye chāpy akṣharam avyaktam teṣhām ke yoga-vittamāḥ

Arjun inquired: Between those who are steadfastly devoted to Your personal form and those who worship the formless Brahman, whom do You consider to be more perfect in Yog?

श्रीभगवानुवाच ।
मय्यावेश्य मनो ये मां नित्ययुक्ता उपासते ।
श्रद्धया परयोपेतास्ते मे युक्ततमा मताः ॥ 2 ॥

shrī-bhagavān uvācha
mayy āveshya mano ye mām nitya-yuktā upāsate
shraddhayā parayopetās te me yuktatamā matāḥ

The Lord said: Those who fix their mind on Me and always engage in My devotion with steadfast faith, I consider them to be the best yogis.

God can be realized in varying degrees of closeness. Let us understand this through an example. Say you are standing by the railway tracks, and a train is coming from afar with its headlight shining. It seems to you as if a light is approaching. When the train comes closer, you can see a shimmering form along with the light. Finally, when it comes and pulls up on the platform in front, you realize, 'Oh! It's a train. I can see all these people sitting inside the compartments and peeping out of the windows.' The same train seemed like a light from afar. As it came closer, it appeared to have a shimmering form along with the light. When it drew even nearer, you realized that it was a train. The train was the same, but on being closer to it, your understanding of its different attributes such as shape, colour, passengers, compartments, doors, and windows grew.

Similarly, God is perfect and complete, and the Possessor of unlimited energies. His personality is replete with divine names, forms, pastimes, virtues, associates, and abodes. However, He is realized in varying levels of closeness as the Brahman (formless all-pervading manifestation of God), the Paramatma (the Supreme Soul seated in the heart of all living beings, distinct from the individual soul), and Bhagavaṇ (the personal manifestation of God that descends upon the earth).

The Bhagavatam states:

vadanti tat tattva vidastattvam yaj-jñānamadvayam

brahmeti paramātmeti bhagavān iti shabdyate (1.2.11)

'The knowers of the Truth have stated that there is only

one Supreme Entity that manifests in three ways in the world—Brahman, Paramatma, and Bhagavan.'

Brahman is the all-pervading form of God which is everywhere. It is full of eternality, knowledge, and bliss. However, in this aspect, God does not manifest His infinite qualities, enchanting personal beauty, and sweet pastimes. He is like a divine light that is *nirgun* (without qualities), *nirvisheṣh* (without attributes), *nirākār* (without form).

Those who follow the path of jnana yog worship this aspect of God. This is a distant realization of God as a formless light, just as the train from far appeared like light.

Paramatma is the aspect of God that is seated in everyone's hearts. In verse 18.61, Shree Krishna states: 'The Supreme Lord dwells in the heart of all living beings, O Arjun. According to their karmas, He directs the wanderings of the souls who are seated on a machine made of material energy.' Residing within, God notes all our thoughts and actions, keeps an account of them, and gives the results at the appropriate time. For every life, He remembers our every thought, word, and deed since we were born.

Just as the train, which appeared as light from afar, was seen as a shimmering form when it came closer, similarly, the realization of the Supreme Entity as Paramatma is a closer realization than Brahman.

Bhagavan is the aspect of God that manifests with a personal form. In this Bhagavan aspect, God manifests all the sweetness of His names, forms, qualities, abodes, pastimes, and associates. These attributes exist in Brahman and Paramatma as well but they remain latent, just as fire is latent in a matchstick and only manifests when struck against the igniting strip of the matchbox. Similarly, as Bhagavan, all the powers and aspects of God's personality, which are latent in other forms, are revealed.

The path of bhakti or devotion leads to the realization of the Supreme Entity in His Bhagavan aspect. This is the closest realization of God, just as the details of a train become visible when it comes and stops in front of the observer. Thus, Shree Krishna answers Arjun's question by clarifying that He considers the devotee of His personal form to be the highest yogi.

ये तु सर्वाणि कर्माणि मयि संन्यस्य मत्पराः ।
अनन्येनैव योगेन मां ध्यायन्त उपासते ॥ 6 ॥

तेषामहं समुद्धर्ता मृत्युसंसारसागरात् ।
भवामि नचिरात्पार्थ मय्यावेशितचेतसाम् ॥ 7 ॥

ye tu sarvāṇi karmāṇi mayi sannyasya mat-parāḥ
ananyenaiva yogena mām dhyāyanta upāsate

teṣhām aham samuddhartā mṛityu-samsāra-sāgarāt
bhavāmi na chirāt pārtha mayy āveshita-chetasām

But those who dedicate all their actions to Me, regarding Me as the Supreme goal, worshipping Me and meditating on Me with exclusive devotion, O Parth, I swiftly deliver them from the ocean of birth and death, for their consciousness is united with Me.

Shree Krishna reiterates that His devotees reach Him quickly. Firstly, with the personal form of God as the object of their devotion, they easily focus their mind and senses upon Him. They engage their tongue and ears in chanting and hearing the divine names of God, their eyes in seeing the image of His divine form, their body in performing actions for His pleasure, their mind in thinking of His wonderful pastimes and virtues, and their intellect in contemplating upon His glories. In this way, they quickly unite their consciousness with God.

Secondly, since such devotees continuously offer their heart in uninterrupted bhakti, God quickly bestows His grace upon them and removes the obstacles on their path. For those who are in communion with Him, He dispels their ignorance with the lamp of knowledge. Thus, God Himself becomes the Saviour of His devotees and delivers them from *mṛityu samsāra sāgarāt* (cycle of life and death).

मय्येव मन आधत्स्व मयि बुद्धिं निवेशय ।
निवसिष्यसि मय्येव अत ऊर्ध्वं न संशयः ॥ 8 ॥

mayy eva mana ādhatsva mayi buddhim niveshaya
nivasiṣhyasi mayy eva ata ūrdhvam na sanshayaḥ

Fix your mind on Me alone and surrender your intellect to Me. Thereupon, you will always live in Me. Of this, there is no doubt.

Having explained that worship of the personal form is better, Shree Krishna now begins to explain how to worship

Him. He asks Arjun to do two things—fix the mind on God and surrender the intellect to Him.

The function of the mind is to create desires, attractions, and aversions. The function of the intellect is to think, analyse, and discriminate. The importance of the mind has been repeatedly stated in the Vedic scriptures:

chetaḥ khalvasya bandhāya muktaye chātmano matam
guṇeṣhu saktam bandhāya ratam vā pumsi muktaye

(Bhagavatam 3.25.15)

'Captivity in maya and liberation from it is determined by the mind. If it is attached to the world, one is in bondage. If the mind is detached from the world, one gets liberated.'

Mere physical devotion is not sufficient; we must absorb the mind in thinking of God because without the engagement of the mind, mere sensory activity is of no value. For example, we hear a sermon with our ears, but if the mind wanders off, we will not know what was said. The words will fall on the ears but they will not register. This shows that without engaging the mind, the work of the senses does not count. Therefore, while noting our karmas, God gives importance to the mental work and not the physical work of the senses.

Even beyond the mind is the intellect. We can only fix the mind upon God when we surrender our intellect to Him. In material pursuits as well, when we face situations beyond the capability of our intellect, we take guidance from a person with superior intellect. For example, if we are involved in a legal case, we take the help of a lawyer. The lawyer instructs us how to handle the interrogation by the opposing lawyer. Having no knowledge of law ourselves, we surrender our intellect and simply do as the lawyer recommends.

In the same way, at present our intellect is subject to many defects. Akrur, who went to get Shree Krishna from Vrindavan to Mathura, describes these imperfections of the intellect in the Bhagavatam (10.40.25): *anityānātma duḥkheṣhu viparyaya matirhyaham* Akrur said: 'Our intellect is strapped with wrong knowledge. Though we are eternal souls, we think of ourselves to be the perishable body. Although all the objects of the world are perishable, we think they will always remain with us, and hence, we are busy accumulating them day and night. And though the pursuit of sensual pleasures only results in misery in the long run, we still chase them in the hope that we will find happiness.' The above three defects of the intellect are called *viparyaya*, or reversals of knowledge under material illusion. If we run our life in accordance with the directions of our intellect, we will not make much progress on the divine path.

Thus, if we wish to achieve spiritual success by attaching the mind to God, we must surrender our intellect and follow His directions. Surrendering the intellect means to think in accordance with the knowledge received from God via the medium of the scriptures and the bona fide guru. Characteristics of a surrendered intellect are described in verse 18.62.

अद्वेष्टा सर्वभूतानां मैत्रः करुण एव च ।
निर्ममो निरहङ्कारः समदुःखसुखः क्षमी ॥ 13 ॥

सन्तुष्टः सततं योगी यतात्मा दृढनिश्चयः ।
मय्यर्पितमनोबुद्धिर्यो मद्भक्तः स मे प्रियः ॥ 14 ॥

adveṣhṭā sarva-bhūtānām maitraḥ karuṇa eva cha
nirmamo nirahankāraḥ sama-duḥkha-sukhaḥ kṣhamī

santuṣhṭaḥ satatam yogī yatātmā dṛiḍha-nishchayaḥ
mayy arpita-mano-buddhir yo mad-bhaktaḥ sa me priyaḥ

Those devotees are very dear to Me who are free from malice towards all living beings, who are friendly and compassionate. They are free from attachment to possessions and egotism, equipoised in happiness and distress, and ever-forgiving. They are ever-content, steadily united with Me in devotion, self-controlled, of firm resolve, and dedicated to Me in mind and intellect.

यस्मान्नोद्विजते लोको लोकान्नोद्विजते च यः ।
हर्षामर्षभयोद्वेगैर्मुक्तो यः स च मे प्रियः ॥ 15 ॥

अनपेक्षः शुचिर्दक्ष उदासीनो गतव्यथः ।
सर्वारम्भपरित्यागी यो मद्भक्तः स मे प्रियः ॥ 16 ॥

यो न हृष्यति न द्वेष्टि न शोचति न काङ् क्षति ।
शुभाशुभपरित्यागी भक्तिमान्यः स मे प्रियः ॥ 17 ॥

yasmān nodvijate loko lokān nodvijate cha yaḥ
harṣhāmarṣha-bhayodvegair mukto yaḥ sa cha me priyaḥ

anapekṣhaḥ shuchir dakṣha udāsīno gata-vyathaḥ
sarvārambha-parityāgī yo mad-bhaktaḥ sa me priyaḥ

yo na hṛiṣhyati na dveṣhṭi na shochati na kāṅkṣhati
shubhāshubha-parityāgī bhaktimān yaḥ sa me priyaḥ

Those who are not a source of annoyance to anyone and who in turn are not agitated by anyone, who are equal in pleasure and pain, and free from fear and anxiety, such devotees of Mine are very dear to Me.

Those who are indifferent to worldly gains, externally and internally pure, skilful, without cares, untroubled, and free from selfishness in all undertakings, such devotees of Mine are very dear to Me.

Those who neither rejoice in mundane pleasures nor despair in worldly sorrows, who neither lament for any loss nor hanker for any gain, who renounce both good and evil deeds, such persons who are full of devotion are very dear to Me.

समः शत्रौ च मित्रे च तथा मानापमानयोः ।
शीतोष्णसुखदुःखेषु समः सङ्ग विवर्जितः ॥ 18 ॥

तुल्यनिन्दास्तुतिर्मौनी सन्तुष्टो येन केनचित् ।
अनिकेतः स्थिरमतिर्भक्तिमान्मे प्रियो नरः ॥ 19 ॥

samaḥ shatrau cha mitre cha tathā mānāpamānayoḥ
shītoṣhṇa-sukha-duḥkheṣhu samaḥ saṅga-vivarjitaḥ

tulya-nindā-stutir maunī santuṣhṭo yena kenachit
aniketaḥ sthira-matir bhaktimān me priyo naraḥ

Those who are alike to friend and foe, equipoised in honour and dishonour, cold and heat, joy and sorrow, and are free from all unfavourable association; those who take praise and reproach alike, who are given to silent contemplation, content with what comes their way, without attachment to the place of residence, whose intellect is firmly fixed in Me, and who are full of devotion to Me, such persons are very dear to Me.

ये तु धर्म्यामृतमिदं यथोक्तं पर्युपासते ।
श्रद्दधाना मत्परमा भक्तास्तेऽतीव मे प्रियाः ॥ 20 ॥

ye tu dharmyāmṛitam idam yathoktam paryupāsate
shraddadhānā mat-paramā bhaktās te 'tīva me priyāḥ

Those who honour this nectar of wisdom declared here, have faith in Me, and are devoted and intent on Me as the supreme goal, they are exceedingly dear to Me.

Shree Krishna concludes the chapter by once again reiterating the supremacy of the path of exclusive devotion to Him. Those who make the Supreme Lord as their goal and cultivate devotion with great faith, imbued with the virtues mentioned in the previous verses, are exceedingly dear to God.

Chapter 13

Kshetra Kshetrajna Vibhag Yog

Yog through Distinguishing the Field and the Knower of the Field

श्रीभगवानुवाच ।
इदं शरीरं कौन्तेय क्षेत्रमित्यभिधीयते ।
एतद्यो वेत्ति तं प्राहुः क्षेत्रज्ञ इति तद्विदः ॥ 2 ॥

shrī-bhagavān uvācha
idam sharīram kaunteya kṣhetram ity abhidhīyate
etad yo vetti tam prāhuḥ kṣhetra-jña iti tad-vidaḥ

The Supreme Divine Lord said: O Arjun, this body is termed as *kṣhetra* (the field of activities), and the one who knows this body is called *kṣhetrajña* (the knower of the field) by the sages who discern the truth about both.

Shree Krishna begins explaining the topic of distinction between the body and spirit. The soul is divine and cannot eat, see, smell, hear, taste, or touch. It does all these works vicariously through the body-mind-intellect mechanism, which is thus termed as the field of activities. A magnet has a magnetic field around it which creates electricity on rapid movement. An electric charge has a force field around it. Here, the body is the receptacle for the activities of the individual. Hence, it is termed as *kṣhetra* (the field of activities).

The soul is distinct from the body-mind-intellect mechanism, but forgetful of its divine nature, it identifies with these material entities. Yet, because it has knowledge of the body, it is called *kṣhetrajña* (knower of the field of the body). This terminology has been given by self-realized sages, who were transcendentally situated at the platform of the soul and perceived their distinct identity as separate from the body.

क्षेत्रज्ञं चापि मां विद्धि सर्वक्षेत्रेषु भारत ।
क्षेत्रक्षेत्रज्ञयोर्ज्ञानं यत्तज्ज्ञानं मतं मम ॥ 3 ॥

kṣhetra-jñam chāpi mām viddhi sarva-kṣhetreṣhu bhārata
kṣhetra-kṣhetrajñayor jñānam yat taj jñānam matam mama

O scion of Bharat, I am also the knower of all the individual fields of activity. The understanding of the body as the field of activities, and the soul and God as the knowers of the field, this I hold to be true knowledge.

The soul is only the knower of the individual field of its own body. Even in this limited context, the soul's knowledge of its field is incomplete. God, as the Supreme Soul in the heart of all living beings, is the knower of the fields of all souls. Further, God's knowledge of each *kṣhetra* is perfect and complete. By explaining these distinctions, Shree Krishna establishes the position of the three entities vis-à-vis each other—the material body, the soul, and the Supreme Soul.

In the second part of the above verse, He gives His definition of knowledge. 'True knowledge is understanding not only of the self, the Supreme Lord, and the physical body, but also of the distinction amongst them.' Thus, a wise one is he who understands that we are the soul and not the body.

महाभूतान्यहङ्कारो बुद्धिरव्यक्तमेव च ।
इन्द्रियाणि दशैकं च पञ्च चेन्द्रियगोचराः ॥ 6 ॥

mahā-bhūtāny ahankāro buddhir avyaktam eva cha
indriyāṇi dashaikam cha pañcha chendriya-gocharāḥ

The field of activities is composed of the five great elements, the ego, the intellect, the unmanifest primordial matter, the eleven senses (five knowledge senses, five working senses, and the mind), and the five objects of the senses.

The 24 elements that constitute the field of activities are: *pañcha-mahābhūta* (the five gross elements—earth, water, fire, air, and space), the *pañch-tanmātrās* (five sense objects—taste, touch, smell, sight, and sound), the five working senses (voice, hands, legs, genitals, and anus), the five knowledge senses (ears, eyes, tongue, skin, and nose), mind, intellect, ego, and *prakṛiti* (the primordial form of the material energy). Shree Krishna uses the word *daśhaikam* (ten plus one) to indicate the 11 senses. In these, He includes the mind along with the five knowledge senses and the five working senses. Previously, in verse 10.22, He had mentioned that amongst the senses He is the mind.

अमानित्वमदम्भित्वमहिंसा क्षान्तिरार्जवम् ।
आचार्योपासनं शौचं स्थैर्यमात्मविनिग्रहः ॥ 8 ॥

इन्द्रियार्थेषु वैराग्यमनहङ्कार एव च ।
जन्ममृत्युजराव्याधिदुःखदोषानुदर्शनम् ॥ 9 ॥

असक्तिरनभिष्वङ्गः पुत्रदारगृहादिषु ।
नित्यं च समचित्तत्वमिष्टानिष्टोपपत्तिषु ॥ 10 ॥

मयि चानन्ययोगेन भक्तिरव्यभिचारिणी ।
विविक्तदेशसेवित्वमरतिर्जनसंसदि ॥ 11 ॥

अध्यात्मज्ञाननित्यत्वं तत्वज्ञानार्थदर्शनम् ।
एतज्ज्ञानमिति प्रोक्तमज्ञानं यदतोऽन्यथा ॥ 12 ॥

amānitvam adambhitvam ahinsā kṣhāntir ārjavam
āchāryopāsanam shaucham sthairyam ātma-vinigrahaḥ

indriyārtheṣhu vairāgyam anahankāra eva cha
janma-mṛityu-jarā-vyādhi-duḥkha-doṣhānudarshanam

asaktir anabhiṣhvaṅgaḥ putra-dāra-gṛihādiṣhu
nityam cha sama-chittatvam iṣhṭāniṣhṭopapattiṣhu

mayi chānanya-yogena bhaktir avyabhichāriṇī
vivikta-desha-sevitvam aratir jana-sansadi

adhyātma-jñāna-nityatvam tattva-jñānārtha-darshanam
etaj jñānam iti proktam ajñānam yad ato 'nyathā

Humbleness; freedom from hypocrisy; non-violence; forgiveness; simplicity; service of the Guru; cleanliness of body and mind; steadfastness; and self-control.

Dispassion towards the objects of the senses; absence of egotism; keeping in mind the evils of birth, disease, old age, and death.

Non-attachment; absence of clinging to spouse, children, home, and so on; even-mindedness amidst desired and undesired events in life.

Constant and exclusive devotion towards Me; an inclination for solitary places and an aversion for mundane society.

Constancy in spiritual knowledge; and philosophical pursuit of the Absolute Truth—all these I declare to be knowledge, and what is contrary to it, I call ignorance.

These five verses describe the virtues, habits, behaviours, and attitudes that purify one's life and illuminate it with the light of knowledge. The opposite of these are vanity, hypocrisy, violence, vengeance, duplicity, disrespect for the Guru, uncleanliness of body and mind, unsteadiness, lack of self-control, longing for sense objects, conceit, entanglement in spouse, children, home, etc. Such dispositions cripple the development of self-knowledge. Thus, Shree Krishna calls them ignorance and darkness.

ज्ञेयं यत्तत्प्रवक्ष्यामि यज्ज्ञात्वामृतमश्नुते ।
अनादिमत्परं ब्रह्म न सत्तन्नासदुच्यते ॥ 13 ॥

सर्वतः पाणिपादं तत्सर्वतोऽक्षिशिरोमुखम् ।
सर्वतः श्रुतिमल्लोके सर्वमावृत्य तिष्ठति ॥ 14 ॥

सर्वेन्द्रियगुणाभासं सर्वेन्द्रियविवर्जितम् ।
असक्तं सर्वभृच्चैव निर्गुणं गुणभोक्तृ च ॥ 15 ॥

बहिरन्तश्च भूतानामचरं चरमेव च ।
सूक्ष्मत्वात्तदविज्ञेयं दूरस्थं चान्तिके च तत् ॥ 16 ॥

अविभक्तं च भूतेषु विभक्तमिव च स्थितम् ।
भूतभर्तृ च तज्ज्ञेयं ग्रसिष्णु प्रभविष्णु च ॥ 17 ॥

ज्योतिषामपि तज्ज्योतिस्तमसः परमुच्यते ।
ज्ञानं ज्ञेयं ज्ञानगम्यं हृदि सर्वस्य विष्ठितम् ॥ 18 ॥

jñeyam yat tat pravakṣhyāmi yaj jñātvāmṛitam ashnute
anādi mat-param brahma na sat tan nāsad uchyate

sarvataḥ pāṇi-pādam tat sarvato 'kṣhi-shiro-mukham
sarvataḥ shrutimal loke sarvam āvṛitya tiṣhṭhati

sarvendriya-guṇābhāsam sarvendriya-vivarjitam
asaktam sarva-bhṛich chaiva nirguṇam guṇa-bhoktṛi cha

bahir antash cha bhūtānām acharam charam eva cha
sūkṣhmatvāt tad avijñeyam dūra-stham chāntike cha tat

avibhaktam cha bhūteṣhu vibhaktam iva cha sthitam
bhūta-bhartṛi cha taj jñeyam grasiṣhṇu prabhaviṣhṇu cha

jyotiṣhām api taj jyotis tamasaḥ param uchyate
jñānam jñeyam jñāna-gamyam hṛidi sarvasya viṣhṭhitam

I shall now reveal to you that which ought to be known, and by knowing which, one attains immortality. It is the beginningless Brahman, which lies beyond existence and non-existence.

Everywhere are His hands and feet, eyes, heads, and faces. His ears too are in all places because He pervades everything in the universe.

Though He perceives all sense-objects, yet He is devoid of the senses. He is unattached to everything, and yet He is the sustainer of all. Although He is without attributes, yet He is the enjoyer of the three modes of material nature.

He exists outside and inside all living beings, those that are moving and not moving. He is subtle, and hence, He is incomprehensible. He is very far, but He is also very near.

He is indivisible, yet He appears to be divided amongst living beings. Know the Supreme Entity to be the Sustainer, Annihilator, and Creator of all beings.

He is the source of light in all luminaries and is entirely beyond the darkness of ignorance. He is knowledge, the object of knowledge, and the goal of knowledge. He dwells within the hearts of all living beings.

The contradictory qualities of God are described in these six verses. We should never fall into the trap of describing or understanding God with our limited knowledge and material senses. He is *kartumakartum anyathā karatum samarthaḥ* 'He can do the possible, the impossible, and the reverse of the possible.' Hence, these should be accepted with faith and the understanding that nothing is impossible for God.

इति क्षेत्रं तथा ज्ञानं ज्ञेयं चोक्तं समासतः ।
मद्भक्त एतद्विज्ञाय मद्भावायोपपद्यते ॥ 19 ॥

iti kṣhetram tathā jñānam jñeyam choktam samāsataḥ
mad-bhakta etad vijñāya mad-bhāvāyopapadyate

I have thus revealed to you the nature of the field, the meaning of knowledge, and the object of knowledge. Only My devotees can understand this in reality, and by doing so, they attain My divine nature.

Having described the field of activity and the knower of this field, Shree Krishna now reiterates the role of devotion in this verse.

उपद्रष्टानुमन्ता च भर्ता भोक्ता महेश्वरः ।
परमात्मेति चाप्युक्तो देहेऽस्मिन्पुरुषः परः ॥ 23 ॥

upadraṣhṭānumantā cha bhartā bhoktā maheshvaraḥ
paramātmeti chāpy ukto dehe 'smin puruṣhaḥ paraḥ

Within the body also resides the Supreme Lord. He is said to be the Witness, the Permitter, the Supporter, the Transcendental Enjoyer, the ultimate Controller, and the Paramatma (Supreme Soul).

य एवं वेत्ति पुरुषं प्रकृतिं च गुणैः सह ।
सर्वथा वर्तमानोऽपि न स भूयोऽभिजायते ॥ 24 ॥

ya evam vetti puruṣham prakṛiti cha guṇaiḥ saha
sarvathā vartamāno 'pi na sa bhūyo 'bhijāyate

Those who understand the truth about Supreme Soul, the individual soul, material nature, and the

interaction of the three modes of nature will not take birth here again. They will be liberated regardless of their present condition.

At the start of this chapter, in verse 13.3, Shree Krishna mentions that true knowledge is that which enables one to understand the body as the field of activities, and the soul and God as knowers of this field. Having described these, He concludes with the same message.

समं सर्वेषु भूतेषु तिष्ठन्तं परमेश्वरम् ।
विनश्यत्स्वविनश्यन्तं यः पश्यति स पश्यति ॥ 28 ॥

समं पश्यन्हि सर्वत्र समवस्थितमीश्वरम् ।
न हिनस्त्यात्मनात्मानं ततो याति परां गतिम् ॥ 29 ॥

यदा भूतपृथग्भावमेकस्थमनुपश्यति ।
तत एव च विस्तारं ब्रह्म सम्पद्यते तदा ॥ 31 ॥

क्षेत्रक्षेत्रज्ञयोरेवमन्तरं ज्ञानचक्षुषा ।
भूतप्रकृतिमोक्षं च ये विदुर्यान्ति ते परम् ॥ 35 ॥

samam sarveṣhu bhūteṣhu tiṣhṭhantam parameshvaram
vinashyatsv avinashyantam yaḥ pashyati sa pashyati

samam paśhyan hi sarvatra samavasthitam īśhvaram
na hinasty ātmanātmānam tato yāti parām gatim

yadā bhūta-pṛithag-bhāvam eka-stham anupaśhyati
tata eva cha vistāram brahma sampadyate tadā

kṣhetra-kṣhetrajñayor evam antaram jñāna-chakṣhuṣhā
bhūta-prakṛiti-mokṣham cha ye vidur yānti te param

They alone truly see, who perceive the Paramatma (Supreme Soul) accompanying the soul in all beings, and who understand both to be imperishable in this perishable body.

Those who see God as the Supreme Soul equally present everywhere and in all living beings, do not degrade themselves by their mind. Thereby, they reach the supreme destination.

When they see the diverse variety of living beings situated in the same material nature and understand all of them to be born from it, they attain the realization of the Brahman.

Those who perceive with the eyes of knowledge the difference between the body and the knower of the body, and the process of release from material nature, attain the supreme destination.

In His customary style, Shree Krishna now winds up the topic of the field and the knower of the field by summing up all that He has said. True knowledge is to know the distinction between the material *kṣhetra* (field of activity) and the spiritual *kṣhetrajña* (knower of the field). Those possessing such discriminative knowledge do not look upon themselves as the material body. They identify with their spiritual nature as souls and tiny parts of God. And as a result, with the eyes of knowledge, they can see the unity in diversity because the Supreme Soul is seated in all.

Chapter 14

Guna Traya Vibhag Yog

Yog through Understanding the Three Modes of Material Nature

सत्त्वं रजस्तम इति गुणाः प्रकृतिसम्भवाः ।
निबध्नन्ति महाबाहो देहे देहिनमव्ययम् ॥ 5 ॥

sattvam rajas tama iti guṇāḥ prakṛiti-sambhavāḥ
nibadhnanti mahā-bāho dehe dehinam avyayam

O mighty-armed Arjun, material energy consists of three gunas (modes)—sattva (goodness), rajas (passion), and tamas (ignorance). These modes bind the eternal soul to the perishable body.

Although the soul is divine, its identification with the body ties it to material nature. Material energy possesses three gunas—sattva, rajas, and tamas. Since the body, mind, and intellect are made from prakriti, they also possess these three modes.

Consider the example of three-colour printing. If any one of the colours is released in excess, then the picture acquires a hue of that colour. Similarly, prakriti has the ink of the three colours. Based on one's internal thoughts, external circumstances, past sanskars, and other factors, one or the other of these modes becomes dominant in that person. And the mode that predominates creates its corresponding shade upon that person's personality. Hence, the soul is swayed by the influence of these dominating modes. Shree Krishna now describes the impact of these modes upon the living being.

तत्र सत्त्वं निर्मलत्वात्प्रकाशकमनामयम् ।
सुखसङ्गेन बध्नाति ज्ञानसङ्गेन चानघ ॥ 6 ॥

tatra sattvam nirmalatvāt prakāshakam anāmayam
sukha-saṅgena badhnāti jñāna-saṅgena chānagha

Amongst these, sattva guna, the mode of goodness, being purer than the others, is illuminating and full of well-being. O sinless one, it binds the soul by creating attachment for a sense of happiness and knowledge.

The word *prakāshakam* means 'illuminating'. The word *anāmayam* means 'healthy and full of well-being'. By extension, it also means 'of peaceful quality' devoid of any inherent cause for pain, discomfort, or misery. The mode of goodness is serene and illuminating. Thus, sattva guna engenders virtues in one's personality and illuminates the intellect with knowledge. It makes a person calm, satisfied, charitable, compassionate, helpful, serene, and tranquil. It also nurtures good health and freedom from sickness. While the mode of goodness creates an effect of serenity and happiness, attachment to them itself binds the soul to material nature.

रजो रागात्मकं विद्धि तृष्णासङ्गसमुद्भवम् ।
तन्निबध्नाति कौन्तेय कर्मसङ्गेन देहिनम् ॥ 7 ॥

rajo rāgātmakam viddhi tṛiṣhṇā-saṅga-samudbhavam
tan nibadhnāti kaunteya karma-saṅgena dehinam

O Arjun, rajo guna is of the nature of passion. It arises from worldly desires and affections and binds the soul through attachment to fruitive actions.

The mode of passion fuels desire for sensual enjoyment. It inflames desires for mental and physical pleasures. It also promotes attachment to worldly things. Persons influenced by rajo guna get engrossed in worldly pursuits of status, prestige, career, family, and home. They look on these as sources of pleasure and are motivated to undertake intense activity for the sake of these. In this way, the mode of passion increases desires, and these desires further fuel an increase of the mode of passion. They both nourish each other and trap the soul in worldly life.

तमस्त्वज्ञानजं विद्धि मोहनं सर्वदेहिनाम् ।
प्रमादालस्यनिद्राभिस्तन्निबध्नाति भारत ॥ 8 ॥

tamas tv ajñāna-jam viddhi mohanam sarva-dehinām
pramādālasya-nidrābhis tan nibadhnāti bhārata

O Arjun, tamo guna, which is born of ignorance, is the cause of illusion for the embodied souls. It deludes all living beings through negligence, laziness, and sleep.

Tamo guna is the antithesis of sattva guna. Persons influenced by it get pleasure through sleep, laziness, intoxication, violence, and gambling. They lose sight of right and wrong, and do not hesitate in resorting to immoral behaviour for fulfilling their desires. Doing their duty becomes burdensome and they neglect it, becoming more inclined to sloth and sleep. In this way, the mode of ignorance leads the soul deeper into the darkness of ignorance. It becomes totally oblivious of its spiritual identity, its goal in life, and the opportunity for progress that the human form provides.

सत्त्वं सुखे सञ्जयति रजः कर्मणि भारत ।
ज्ञानमावृत्य तु तमः प्रमादे सञ्जयत्युत ॥ 9 ॥

sattvam sukhe sañjayati rajaḥ karmaṇi bhārata
jñānam āvṛitya tu tamaḥ pramāde sañjayaty uta

Sattva binds one to material happiness; rajas conditions the soul towards actions; and tamas clouds wisdom and binds one to delusion.

In the mode of goodness, the miseries of material existence reduce and worldly desires become subdued. This gives rise to a feeling of contentment with one's condition. However, those in goodness can easily become complacent and feel no urge to progress to the transcendental platform. Also, sattva guna illumines the intellect with knowledge. If this is not accompanied by spiritual wisdom, then knowledge results in pride and that pride comes in the way of devotion to God.

In the mode of passion, the souls are impelled towards intense activity. Their attachment to the world and preference for pleasure, prestige, wealth, and bodily comforts propels them to work hard for achieving these goals, which they consider to be the most important in life.

The mode of ignorance clouds the intellect of the living being. The desire for happiness now manifests in perverse behaviours, such as addiction or violence.

सर्वद्वारेषु देहेऽस्मिन्प्रकाश उपजायते ।
ज्ञानं यदा तदा विद्याद्विवृद्धं सत्त्वमित्युत ॥ 11 ॥

लोभ: प्रवृत्तिरारम्भ: कर्मणामशम: स्पृहा ।
रजस्येतानि जायन्ते विवृद्धे भरतर्षभ ॥ 12 ॥

अप्रकाशोऽप्रवृत्तिश्च प्रमादो मोह एव च ।
तमस्येतानि जायन्ते विवृद्धे कुरुनन्दन ॥ 13 ॥

sarva-dvāreṣhu dehe 'smin prakāsha upajāyate
jñānam yadā tadā vidyād vivṛiddham sattvam ity uta

lobhaḥ pravṛittir ārambhaḥ karmaṇām ashamaḥ spṛihā
rajasy etāni jāyante vivṛiddhe bharatarṣhabha

aprakāsho 'pravṛittish cha pramādo moha eva cha
tamasy etāni jāyante vivṛiddhe kuru-nandana

When all the gates of the body are illumined by knowledge, know it to be a manifestation of the mode of goodness.

When the mode of passion predominates, O Arjun, the symptoms of greed, exertion for worldly gain, restlessness, and craving develop.

O Arjun, nescience, inertia, negligence, and delusion—these are the dominant signs of the mode of ignorance.

Shree Krishna once again repeats how the three modes influence one's thinking. Sattva guna leads to the development of virtues and the illumination of knowledge. Rajo guna leads to greed, inordinate activity for worldly attainments, and restlessness of the mind. Tamo guna results in delusion of the intellect, laziness, and inclination towards intoxication and violence.

For the mind to fluctuate due to the three gunas is very natural. However, we are not to be dejected by this state of affairs, rather, we should understand why it happens and work to rise above it. Sadhana means to fight with the flow of the three gunas in the mind and force it to maintain the devotional feelings towards God and Guru. If our consciousness remained at the highest level all day, there would be no need for sadhana. Though the mind's natural sentiments may be inclined towards the world, yet with the intellect, we have to force it into the spiritual realm. At first, this may seem hard but with practice it becomes easy. This is just as driving a car is initially difficult but becomes natural with practice.

नान्यं गुणेभ्यः कर्तारं यदा द्रष्टानुपश्यति ।
गुणेभ्यश्च परं वेत्ति मद्भावं सोऽधिगच्छति ॥ 19 ॥

nānyam guṇebhyaḥ kartāram yadā draṣhṭānupashyati
guṇebhyash cha param vetti mad-bhāvam so 'dhigachchhati

When wise persons see that in all work there is no agent of action other than the three gunas, and they know Me to be transcendental to these gunas, they attain My divine nature.

Having revealed the complex workings of the three gunas, Shree Krishna now shows the simple solution for breaking out of their bondage. All the living entities in the world are under the grip of the three gunas, and hence the gunas are the active agents in all the works being done in the world. But the Supreme Lord is beyond them; He is called *tri-guṇātīt* (transcendental to the modes of material nature). Similarly, all the attributes of God—His names, forms, virtues, pastimes, abodes, saints—are also *tri-guṇātīt*.

If we attach our mind to any personality or object within the realm of the three gunas, it results in increasing their corresponding colour on our mind and intellect. However, if we attach our mind to the divine realm, it transcends the gunas and becomes divine. Those who understand this principle start releasing their relationship with worldly objects and people, and strengthening it, through bhakti, with God and the Guru. This enables them to transcend the three gunas and attain the Divine.

श्रीभगवानुवाच ।
प्रकाशं च प्रवृत्तिं च मोहमेव च पाण्डव ।
न द्वेष्टि सम्प्रवृत्तानि न निवृत्तानि काङ् क्षति ॥ 22 ॥

उदासीनवदासीनो गुणैर्यो न विचाल्यते ।
गुणा वर्तन्त इत्येवं योऽवतिष्ठति नेङ्गते ॥ 23 ॥

shrī-bhagavān uvācha
prakāsham cha pravṛittim cha moham eva cha pāṇḍava
na dveṣhṭi sampravṛittāni na nivṛittāni kāṅkṣhati

udāsīna-vad āsīno guṇair yo na vichālyate
guṇā vartanta ity evam yo 'vatiṣhṭhati neṅgate

The Supreme Divine Personality said: O Arjun, The persons who are transcendental to the three gunas neither hate illumination (which is born of sattva), nor activity (which is born of rajas), nor even delusion (which is born of tamas), when these are abundantly present, nor do they long for them when they are absent. They remain neutral to the modes of nature and are not disturbed by them. Knowing it is only the gunas that act, they stay established in the self, without wavering.

Shree Krishna now clarifies the traits of those who have transcended the three gunas. They are not disturbed when they see the gunas functioning in the world, and their effects manifesting in persons, objects, and situations around them. Illumined persons do not hate ignorance when they see it, nor do they get implicated in it. The enlightened souls also strive for human welfare, but they do so because it is their nature to help others. At the same time, they realize that they simply have to do their duty to the best of their ability and leave the rest in the hands of God. Having come into God's world, our first duty is to purify ourself. Then, with a pure mind, we will naturally do good and beneficial works in the world, without allowing worldly situations to bear too heavily upon us.

Shree Krishna explains that persons of illumination, who know themselves to be transcendental to the functioning of the modes, are neither miserable nor jubilant when the modes of nature perform their natural functions in the world. In fact, even when they perceive these gunas in their mind, they do not get disturbed. Persons on the transcendental platform fix their mind in God alone and stand steadfast.

समदुःखसुखः स्वस्थः समलोष्टाश्मकाञ्चनः ।
तुल्यप्रियाप्रियो धीरस्तुल्यनिन्दात्मसंस्तुतिः ॥ 24 ॥

मानापमानयोस्तुल्यस्तुल्यो मित्रारिपक्षयोः ।
सर्वारम्भपरित्यागी गुणातीतः स उच्यते ॥ 25 ॥

sama-duḥkha-sukhaḥ sva-sthaḥ sama-loṣhṭāshma-kāñchanaḥ
tulya-priyāpriyo dhīras tulya-nindātma-sanstutiḥ

mānāpamānayos tulyas tulyo mitrāri-pakṣhayoḥ
sarvārambha-parityāgī guṇātītaḥ sa uchyate

Those who are alike in happiness and distress; who are established in the self; who look upon a clod, a stone, and a piece of gold as of equal value; who remain the same amidst pleasant and unpleasant events; who are intelligent; who accept both blame and praise with equanimity.

Those who remain the same in honour and dishonour; who treat both friend and foe alike; and who have abandoned all enterprises—they are said to have risen above the three gunas.

मां च योऽव्यभिचारेण भक्तियोगेन सेवते ।
स गुणान्समतीत्यैतान्ब्रह्मभूयाय कल्पते ॥ 26 ॥

mām cha yo 'vyabhichāreṇa bhakti-yogena sevate
sa guṇān samatītyaitān brahma-bhūyāya kalpate

Those who serve Me with unalloyed devotion rise above the three modes of material nature and come to the level of Brahman.

Having explained the traits of those who are situated beyond the three gunas, Shree Krishna now reveals the one and only method of transcending these modes of material nature. The verse indicates that mere knowledge of the self and its distinction with the body is not enough. With the help of bhakti yog, the mind has to be fixed on the Supreme Lord, Shree Krishna. Then alone will the mind become *nirgun* (untouched by the three modes), just as Shree Krishna is *nirgun*.

Many people are of the view that if the mind is fixed upon the personal form of God, it will not rise to the transcendental platform. Only when it is attached to the formless Brahman, will the mind become transcendental to the modes of material nature. However, this verse refutes such a view. Although the personal form of God possesses infinite gunas (qualities), these are all divine and beyond the modes of material nature. Hence, the personal form of God is also *nirgun* (beyond the three material modes).

This verse also reveals the proper object of meditation. Transcendental meditation does not mean to meditate upon nothingness. The entity transcendental to the three modes of material nature is God. So, only when the object of our meditation is God can it truly be called transcendental meditation.

Chapter 15

Purushottam Yog

The Yog of the Supreme Divine Personality

श्रीभगवानुवाच ।
ऊर्ध्वमूलमधःशाखमश्वत्थं प्राहुरव्ययम् ।
छन्दांसि यस्य पर्णानि यस्तं वेद स वेदवित् ॥ 1 ॥

shrī-bhagavān uvācha
ūrdhva-mūlam adhaḥ-shākham ashvattham prāhur avyayam
chhandānsi yasya parṇāni yas tam veda sa veda-vit

The Supreme Divine Personality said: They speak of an eternal *ashvatth* tree with its roots above and branches below. Its leaves are the Vedic hymns, and one who knows the secret of this tree is the knower of the Vedas.

The word *ashvatth* means that which will not remain the same until even the next day. This world is also *ashvatth* because it is constantly changing. The Sanskrit dictionary defines the world in the following manner: *sansaratīti sansāraḥ* 'that which is constantly shifting is *sansar* (a Sanskrit word for world).' *Gachchhatīti jagat* 'that which is always moving is *jagat* (another Sanskrit word for world).' Not only is the world always changing, but it will also be annihilated and absorbed back into God one day. Thus, everything in it is temporary or *ashvatth*.

Ashvatth also has another meaning. It is the peepal (sacred fig) tree of the banyan family. Shree Krishna explains that for the soul, this material world is like a huge *ashvatth* tree. Generally, trees have their roots below and branches above. But this tree has its roots above (*ūrdhva-mūlam*), i.e. it originated from God, is based in Him, and is supported by Him. Its trunk and branches extend downward (*adhaḥ-shākham*), encompassing all life-forms in all the abodes of the material realm.

The leaves of the tree are those Vedic mantras (*chhandānsi*) that deal with ritualistic ceremonies and their rewards. They provide the juice for nourishing the tree of material existence. By engaging in the fruitive ritualistic yajnas described in these Vedic mantras, the soul goes to the heavenly abodes to enjoy celestial pleasures, only to descend back to earth when the meritorious deeds are depleted. Thus, the leaves of the tree nourish it by perpetuating the cycle of life and death.

This tree in the form of the world is called eternal (*avyayam*) because its flow is continuous, and its beginning and end are not experienced by the souls. Just as the water of the sea evaporates to form clouds, then rains down on earth and merges into the sea again in a continuous process, similarly, the cycle of life and death is also perpetual.

अधश्चोर्ध्वं प्रसृतास्तस्य शाखा
गुणप्रवृद्धा विषयप्रवालाः ।
अधश्च मूलान्यनुसन्ततानि
कर्मानुबन्धीनि मनुष्यलोके ॥ 2 ॥

adhash chordhvam prasṛitās tasya shākhā
guṇa-pravṛiddhā viṣhaya-pravālāḥ
adhash cha mūlāny anusantatāni
karmānubandhīni manuṣhya-loke

The branches of the tree extend upward and downward, nourished by the three gunas, with the objects of the senses as tender buds. The roots of the tree hang downward, causing the flow of karma in the human form. Below, its roots branch out causing (karmic) actions in the world of humans.

Shree Krishna continues comparing the material creation with the *ashvatth* tree. The main trunk of the tree is the human form in which the soul performs karmas. The branches (*shākhās*) of the tree extend both downward (*adhaḥ*) and upward (*ūrddhva*). If the soul commits sinful activities, it is reborn either in the animal species or in the nether regions. These are the downward branches. If the soul performs virtuous acts, it is reborn in the celestial abodes as a *gandharva, devata*, or another being in those abodes. These are the upward branches.

As a tree is irrigated by water, this tree of material existence is irrigated by the three modes of material nature. These three modes generate sense objects that are like the buds on the tree (*viṣhaya-pravālāḥ*). The function of buds is to sprout and cause further growth. The buds on this *ashvatth* tree sprout and create material desires that are like the aerial roots of the tree.

न रूपमस्येह तथोपलभ्यते
नान्तो न चादिर्न च सम्प्रतिष्ठा ।
अश्वत्थमेनं सुविरूढमूल
मसङ्गशस्त्रेण दृढेन छित्त्वा ॥ 3 ॥

ततः पदं तत्परिमार्गितव्यं
यस्मिन्गता न निवर्तन्ति भूयः ।
तमेव चाद्यं पुरुषं प्रपद्ये
यतः प्रवृत्तिः प्रसृता पुराणी ॥ 4 ॥

na rūpam asyeha tathopalabhyate
nānto na chādir na cha sampratiṣhṭhā
ashvattham enam su-virūḍha-mūlam
asaṅga-shastreṇa dṛiḍhena chhittvā

tataḥ padam tat parimārgitavyam
yasmin gatā na nivartanti bhūyaḥ
tam eva chādyam puruṣham prapadye
yataḥ pravṛittiḥ prasṛitā purāṇī

The real form of this tree is not perceived in this world, neither its beginning, nor end, nor its continued existence. But this deep-rooted *ashvatth* tree must be cut down with a strong axe of detachment. Then one must search out the base of the tree, which is the Supreme Lord, from Whom streamed forth the activity of the universe a long time ago. Upon taking refuge in Him, one will not return to this world again.

The embodied souls immersed in samsara, or the perpetual cycle of life and death, are unable to comprehend the nature of this *ashvatth* tree. They find the buds of the tree to be very attractive, i.e. they are lured by the objects of the senses and develop desires for them. To fulfil these desires, they undertake great endeavours without realizing that their efforts only nourish the tree to grow even further.

Shree Krishna explains that this riddle of the *ashvatth* tree is understood only by a few. Not comprehending the origin and nature of the tree, the living being engages in worthless actions. Sometimes, the propensity for material enjoyment attracts one to the leaves of the tree, which are the ritualistic ceremonies of the Vedas. By engaging in these activities, one goes upward to the celestial abodes, only to come back again when the pious merits are depleted.

Shree Krishna says that the axe to cut this tree is dispassion. The word *asaṅg* means detachment, and it is the remedy for the soul's endless miseries. When one develops detachment, further growth of the tree stops, and it starts withering.

We must then search for the base of this tree, which is situated above the roots and is higher than everything else. That base is the Supreme Lord, as Shree Krishna previously stated: 'I am the Origin of all creation. Everything proceeds from Me. The wise who know this perfectly worship Me with great faith and devotion.' (verse 10.8) Thus, finding the original source of the tree, we must surrender to it in the manner described in this verse. Then, on taking refuge of the Supreme Lord, the *ashvatth* tree will be cut. We will not have to return to this world again and will go to His divine abode after death.

यदादित्यगतं तेजो जगद्भासयतेऽखिलम् ।
यच्चन्द्रमसि यच्चाग्नौ तत्तेजो विद्धि मामकम् ॥ 12 ॥

गामाविश्य च भूतानि धारयाम्यहमोजसा ।
पुष्णामि चौषधीः सर्वाः सोमो भूत्वा रसात्मकः ॥ 13 ॥

अहं वैश्वानरो भूत्वा प्राणिनां देहमाश्रितः ।
प्राणापानसमायुक्तः पचाम्यन्नं चतुर्विधम् ॥ 14 ॥

yad āditya-gatam tejo jagad bhāsayate 'khilam
yach chandramasi yach chāgnau tat tejo viddhi māmakam

gām āviśhya cha bhūtāni dhārayāmy aham ojasā
puṣhṇāmi chauṣhadhīḥ sarvāḥ somo bhūtvā rasātmakaḥ

aham vaiśhvānaro bhūtvā prāṇinām deham āśhritaḥ
prāṇāpāna-samāyuktaḥ pachāmy annam chatur-vidham

Know that I am like the brilliance of the sun that illuminates the entire solar system. The radiance of the moon and the brightness of the fire also come from Me.

Permeating the earth, I nourish all living beings with My energy. Becoming the moon, I nourish all plants with the juice of life.

It is I who take the form of the fire of digestion in the stomachs of all living beings, and combine with the incoming and outgoing breaths, to digest and assimilate the four kinds of foods.

In these three verses Shree Krishna reveals that He is the source of life in various forms. He is the sunlight without which life would not be possible. He is the moonlight which provides nourishment to all plants. He is the fire of digestion in all living beings who would starve without food and nutrients to sustain the body.

In other words, He alone makes all aspects of life possible. He energizes the earth to make it hospitable. He energizes the moon to nourish all vegetation. He becomes the gastric fire to digest the four kinds of food.

सर्वस्य चाहं हृदि सन्निविष्टो
मत्तः स्मृतिर्ज्ञानमपोहनं च ।
वेदैश्च सर्वैरहमेव वेद्यो
वेदान्तकृद्वेदविदेव चाहम् ॥ 15 ॥

sarvasya chāham hṛidi sanniviṣhṭo
mattaḥ smṛitir jñānam apohanam cha
vedaish cha sarvair aham eva vedyo
vedānta-kṛid veda-vid eva chāham

I am seated in the hearts of all living beings and from Me come memory, knowledge, as well as forgetfulness. I alone am to be known by all the Vedas, am the author of the Vedant, and the knower of the meaning of the Vedas.

Shree Krishna reiterates that He is seated in all as Paramatma who notes all our actions and bestows results accordingly.

The qualities of memory, knowledge, and forgetfulness also stem from Him. He determines the intensity and extent (scope) of these, which is why they differ in all.

For example, some have amazing memories like an elephant while others forget the simplest things, such as where they last left their keys or eyeglasses.

The Vedas manifested from God, Who is free from all defects. This means that the Vedas are credible and trustworthy. Additionally, since God is divine and our senses, mind, and intellect are material, we cannot understand Him or His creation. Ved Vyas, who was an Avatar of God, wrote the *Vedant Darshan*. This means that Shree Krishna is the author of the *Vedant* as well.

Vedas are considered the authority on the principles of how to live our life, and the essence of all Vedic scriptures is to know and love God. Thus, He alone is the goal of all knowledge.

In this manner, Shree Krishna is emphasizing that He alone is the source of knowledge, the means of knowledge, and the goal of knowledge.

यो मामेवमसम्मूढो जानाति पुरुषोत्तमम् ।
स सर्वविद्भजति मां सर्वभावेन भारत ॥ 19 ॥

इति गुह्यतमं शास्त्रमिदमुक्तं मयानघ ।
एतद्बुद्ध्वा बुद्धिमान्स्यात्कृतकृत्यश्च भारत ॥ 20 ॥

yo mām evam asammūḍho jānāti puruṣhottamam
sa sarva-vid bhajati mām sarva-bhāvena bhārata

iti guhyatamam shāstram idam uktam mayānagha
etad buddhvā buddhimān syāt kṛita-kṛityash cha bhārata

Those who know Me without doubt as the Supreme Divine Personality truly have complete knowledge. O Arjun, they worship Me with their whole being.

I have shared this most secret principle of the Vedic scriptures with you, O sinless Arjun. By understanding this, a person becomes enlightened and fulfils all that is to be accomplished.

Shree Krishna concludes this chapter by reiterating the message of devotion to the Supreme Divine Personality, knowing which nothing more is left to be known and nothing more is to be done.

Chapter 16

Daivasura Sampad Vibhag Yog

Yog through Discerning the Divine and Demoniac Natures

श्रीभगवानुवाच ।
अभयं सत्त्वसंशुद्धिर्ज्ञानयोगव्यवस्थितिः ।
दानं दमश्च यज्ञश्च स्वाध्यायस्तप आर्जवम् ॥ 1 ॥

अहिंसा सत्यमक्रोधस्त्यागः शान्तिरपैशुनम् ।
दया भूतेष्वलोलुप्त्वं मार्दवं ह्रीरचापलम् ॥ 2 ॥

तेजः क्षमा धृतिः शौचमद्रोहोनातिमानिता ।
भवन्ति सम्पदं दैवीमभिजातस्य भारत ॥ 3 ॥

shrī-bhagavān uvācha
abhayam sattva-sanshuddhir jñāna-yoga-vyavasthitiḥ
dānam damash cha yajñash cha svādhyāyas tapa ārjavam

ahinsā satyam akrodhas tyāgaḥ shāntir apaishunam
dayā bhūteṣhv aloluptvam mārdavam hrīr achāpalam

tejaḥ kṣhamā dhṛitiḥ shaucham adroho nāti-mānitā
bhavanti sampadam daivīm abhijātasya bhārata

The Supreme Divine Personality said: O scion of Bharat, these are the saintly virtues of those endowed with a divine nature—fearlessness, purity of mind, steadfastness in spiritual knowledge, charity, control of the senses, sacrifice, study of the sacred books, austerity, and straightforwardness; non-violence, truthfulness, absence of anger, renunciation,

peacefulness, restraint from fault-finding, compassion towards all living beings, absence of covetousness, gentleness, modesty, and lack of fickleness; vigour, forgiveness, fortitude, cleanliness, bearing enmity towards none, and absence of vanity.

दम्भो दर्पोऽभिमानश्च क्रोधः पारुष्यमेव च ।
अज्ञानं चाभिजातस्य पार्थ सम्पदमासुरीम् ॥ 4 ॥

प्रवृत्तिं च निवृत्तिं च जना न विदुरासुराः ।
न शौचं नापि चाचारो न सत्यं तेषु विद्यते ॥ 7 ॥

चिन्तामपरिमेयां च प्रलयान्तामुपाश्रिताः ।
कामोपभोगपरमा एतावदिति निश्चिताः ॥ 11 ॥

dambho darpo 'bhimānash cha krodhaḥ pārușhyam eva cha
ajñānam chābhijātasya pārtha sampadam āsurīm

pravṛittim cha nivṛittim cha janā na vidur āsurāḥ
na śhaucham nāpi chāchāro na satyam teṣhu vidyate

chintām aparimeyām cha pralayāntām upāshritāḥ
kāmopabhoga-paramā etāvad iti nishchitāḥ

O Parth, the qualities of those who possess a demoniac nature are hypocrisy, arrogance, conceit, anger, harshness, and ignorance.

Those possessing a demoniac nature do not comprehend which actions are proper and which are improper. Hence, they possess neither purity, nor good conduct, nor even truthfulness.

They are obsessed with endless anxieties that end only with death. Still, they maintain with complete assurance that gratification of desires and accumulation of wealth is the highest purpose of life.

त्रिविधं नरकस्येदं द्वारं नाशनमात्मनः ।
कामः क्रोधस्तथा लोभस्तस्मादेतत्त्रयं त्यजेत् ॥ 21 ॥

एतैर्विमुक्तः कौन्तेय तमोद्वारैस्त्रिभिर्नरः ।
आचरत्यात्मनः श्रेयस्ततो याति परां गतिम् ॥ 22 ॥

tri-vidham narakasyedam dvāram nāshanam ātmanaḥ
kāmaḥ krodhas-tathā lobhas-tasmād-etat-trayam tyajet

etair vimuktaḥ kaunteya tamo-dvārais tribhir naraḥ
ācharaty ātmanaḥ shreyas tato yāti parām gatim

There are three gates leading to the hell of self-destruction for the soul—lust, anger, and greed. Therefore, one should abandon all three.

Those who are free from the three gates to darkness endeavour for the welfare of their soul and thereby attain the supreme goal.

Shree Krishna now describes the origin of the demoniac disposition and pinpoints desire, anger, and greed as the three causes for it. Previously, Arjun had asked Him why people are impelled to commit sin, even unwillingly, as if by force. Shree Krishna had answered that it is desire, which later transforms into anger and is the all-devouring enemy of the world. Greed is also a transformation of desire, as mentioned in verse 2.62. Together, desire, anger, and greed are the foundations from which demoniac vices develop. They fester in the mind and make it a suitable ground for all other vices to take root. Consequently, Shree Krishna labels them as gateways to hell and strongly advises to shun them to avoid self-destruction.

Those desirous of welfare should learn to dread these three and carefully avoid their presence in their own personality. And when they learn to do so, they traverse the spiritual path quickly to eventually reach the supreme destination.

तस्माच्छात्रं प्रमाणं ते कार्याकार्यव्यवस्थितौ ।
ज्ञात्वा शास्त्रविधानोक्तं कर्म कर्तुमिहार्हसि ॥ 24 ॥

tasmāch-chhāstram pramāṇam te kāryākārya-vyavasthitau
jñātvā shāstra-vidhānoktam karma kartum ihārhasi

Therefore, let the scriptures be your authority in determining what should be done and what should not be done. Understand the scriptural injunctions and teachings, and then perform your actions in this world accordingly.

Shree Krishna now gives the final conclusion of the teachings in this chapter. By comparing and differentiating between divine and demoniac natures, He highlights how the demoniac nature leads to hellish existence and that nothing is to be gained by discarding the injunctions of the scriptures. Now He drives home the point by stating that the absolute authority in ascertaining the propriety of any activity, or lack of it, are the Vedic scriptures. Hence, Shree Krishna concludes by instructing Arjun to comprehend the teachings of the scriptures and act according to them.

Chapter 17

Shraddha Traya Vibhag Yog

Yog through Discerning the Three Divisions of Faith

आहारस्त्वपि सर्वस्य त्रिविधो भवति प्रियः ।
यज्ञस्तपस्तथा दानं तेषां भेदमिमं श्रृणु ॥ 7 ॥

āhāras tv api sarvasya tri-vidho bhavati priyaḥ
yajñas tapas tathā dānam teṣhām bhedam imam shṛiṇu

The food that people prefer is according to their dispositions. The same is true for sacrifice, austerity, and charity they are inclined (or predisposed) to. Now hear of the distinctions from Me.

This verse serves as the introduction for the topics Shree Krishna is going to discuss in this chapter. Using the three material gunas as the lens, He starts by explaining the nature of food and sacrifice. Shree Krishna then shares a brief definition of austerity of body, speech, and mind, and continues to explain their natures. Finally, He reveals the nature of charity.

आयुःसत्त्वबलारोग्यसुखप्रीतिविवर्धनाः ।
रस्याः स्निग्धाः स्थिरा हृद्या आहाराः सात्त्विकप्रियाः ॥ 8 ॥

कट्वम्ललवणात्युष्णतीक्ष्णरूक्षविदाहिनः ।
आहारा राजसस्येष्टा दुःखशोकामयप्रदाः ॥ 9 ॥

यातयामं गतरसं पूति पर्युषितं च यत् ।
उच्छिष्टमपि चामेध्यं भोजनं तामसप्रियम् ॥ 10 ॥

āyuḥ-sattva-balārogya-sukha-prīti-vivardhanāḥ
rasyāḥ snigdhāḥ sthirā hṛidyā āhārāḥ sāttvika-priyāḥ

kaṭv-amla-lavaṇāty-uṣhṇa- tīkṣhṇa-rūkṣha-vidāhinaḥ
āhārā rājasasyeṣhṭā duḥkha-shokāmaya-pradāḥ

yāta-yāmam gata-rasam pūti paryuṣhitam cha yat
uchchhiṣhṭam api chāmedhyam bhojanam tāmasa-priyam

Persons in the mode of goodness prefer foods that promote lifespan, and increase virtue, strength, health, happiness, and satisfaction. Such foods are juicy, succulent, nourishing, and naturally tasteful.

Foods that are too bitter, too sour, salty, very hot, pungent, dry, and full of chillies, are dear to persons in the mode of passion. Such foods produce pain, grief, and disease.

Foods that are overcooked, stale, putrid, polluted, and impure are dear to persons in the mode of ignorance.

अफलाकाङ्क्षिभिर्यज्ञो विधिदृष्टो य इज्यते ।
यष्टव्यमेवेति मनः समाधाय स सात्त्विकः ॥ 11 ॥

अभिसन्धाय तु फलं दम्भार्थमपि चैव यत् ।
इज्यते भरतश्रेष्ठ तं यज्ञं विद्धि राजसम् ॥ 12 ॥

विधिहीनमसृष्टान्नं मन्त्रहीनमदक्षिणम् ।
श्रद्धाविरहितं यज्ञं तामसं परिचक्षते ॥ 13 ॥

aphalākāṅkṣhibhir yajño vidhi-driṣhṭo ya ijyate
yaṣhṭavyam eveti manaḥ samādhāya sa sāttvikaḥ

abhisandhāya tu phalam dambhārtham api chaiva yat
ijyate bharata-sshreṣhṭha tam yajñam viddhi rājasam

vidhi-hīnam asṛiṣhṭānnam mantra-hīnam adakṣhiṇam
shraddhā-virahitam yajñam tāmasam parichakṣhate

Sacrifice that is performed according to scriptural injunctions without expectation of rewards, with the firm conviction of the mind that it is a matter of duty, is of the nature of goodness.

O best of the Bharatas, know that sacrifice performed for material benefit or with a hypocritical aim, is in the mode of passion.

Sacrifice devoid of faith and contrary to the injunctions of the scriptures, in which no food is offered, no mantras chanted, and no donation made, is to be considered in the mode of ignorance.

देवद्विजगुरुप्राज्ञपूजनं शौचमार्जवम् ।
ब्रह्मचर्यमहिंसा च शारीरं तप उच्यते ॥ 14 ॥

अनुद्वेगकरं वाक्यं सत्यं प्रियहितं च यत् ।
स्वाध्यायाभ्यसनं चैव वाङ्मयं तप उच्यते ॥ 15 ॥

मनः प्रसादः सौम्यत्वं मौनमात्मविनिग्रहः ।
भावसंशुद्धिरित्येतत्तपो मानसमुच्यते ॥ 16 ॥

deva-dwija-guru-prājña-pūjanam shaucham ārjavam
brahmacharyam ahinsā cha shārīram tapa uchyate

anudvega-karam vākyam satyam priya-hitam cha yat
svādhyāyābhyasanam chaiva vāṅ-mayam tapa uchyate

manaḥ-prasādaḥ saumyatvam maunam ātma-vinigrahaḥ
bhāva-sanshuddhir-ity-etat-tapo mānasam uchyate

When worship of the Supreme Lord, the Brahmins, the spiritual master, the wise, and the elders is done with the observance of cleanliness, simplicity, celibacy, and non-violence, then this worship is declared as the austerity of the body.

Words that do not cause distress, are truthful, inoffensive, and beneficial, as well as regular recitation of the Vedic scriptures—these are declared as austerity of speech.

Serenity of thought, gentleness, silence, self-control, and purity of purpose—all these are declared as austerity of the mind.

श्रद्धया परया तप्तं तपस्तत्त्रिविधं नरैः ।
अफलाकाङ्क्षिभिर्युक्तैः सात्त्विकं परिचक्षते ॥ 17 ॥

सत्कारमानपूजार्थं तपो दम्भेन चैव यत् ।
क्रियते तदिह प्रोक्तं राजसं चलमध्रुवम् ॥ 18 ॥

मूढग्राहेणात्मनो यत्पीडया क्रियते तपः ।
परस्योत्सादनार्थं वा तत्तामसमुदाहृतम् ॥ 19 ॥

shraddhayā parayā taptam tapas tat tri-vidham naraiḥ
aphalākāṅkṣhibhir yuktaiḥ sāttvikam parichakṣhate

satkāra-māna-pūjārtham tapo dambhena chaiva yat
kriyate tad iha proktam rājasam chalam adhruvam

mūḍha-grāheṇātmano yat pīḍayā kriyate tapaḥ
parasyotsādanārtham vā tat tāmasam udāhṛitam

When devout persons with ardent faith practise these three-fold austerities without yearning for material rewards, they are designated as austerities in the mode of goodness.

Austerity that is performed with ostentation for the sake of gaining honour, respect, and adoration is in the mode of passion. Its benefits are unstable and transitory.

Austerity that is performed by those with confused notions and which involves torturing the self or harming others, is described to be in the mode of ignorance.

दातव्यमिति यद्दानं दीयतेऽनुपकारिणे ।
देशे काले च पात्रे च तद्दानं सात्त्विकं स्मृतम् ॥ 20 ॥

यत्तु प्रत्युपकारार्थं फलमुद्दिश्य वा पुनः ।
दीयते च परिक्लिष्टं तद्दानं राजसं स्मृतम् ॥ 21 ॥

अदेशकाले यद्दानमपात्रेभ्यश्च दीयते ।
असत्कृतमवज्ञातं तत्तामसमुदाहृतम् ॥ 22 ॥

dātavyam iti yad dānam dīyate 'nupakāriṇe
deshe kāle cha pātre cha tad dānam sāttvikam smṛitam

yat tu pratyupakārārtham phalam uddiśhya vā punaḥ
dīyate cha parikliṣhṭam tad dānam rājasam smṛitam

adesha-kāle yad dānam apātrebhyash cha dīyate
asat-kṛitam avajñātam tat tāmasam udāhṛitam

Charity given to a worthy person simply because it is right to give, without consideration of anything in return, at the proper time and in the proper place, is stated to be in the mode of goodness.

But charity given with reluctance, with the hope of a return or in expectation of a reward, is said to be in the mode of passion.

And that charity, which is given at the wrong place and wrong time to unworthy persons, without showing respect, or with contempt, is held to be of the nature of nescience.

Chapter 18

Moksha Sanyas Yog

Yog through the Perfection of Renunciation and Surrender

यज्ञदानतपःकर्म न त्याज्यं कार्यमेव तत् ।
यज्ञो दानं तपश्चैव पावनानि मनीषिणाम् ॥ 5 ॥

एतान्यपि तु कर्माणि संङ्ग त्यक्त्वा फलानि च ।
कर्तव्यानीति मे पार्थ निश्चितं मतमुत्तमम् ॥ 6 ॥

yajña-dāna-tapaḥ-karma na tyājyam kāryam-eva tat
yajño dānam tapash chaiva pāvanāni manīṣhiṇām

etāny api tu karmāṇi saṅgam tyaktvā phalāni cha
kartavyānīti me pārtha niśhchitam matam uttamam

Actions based upon sacrifice, charity, and penance should never be abandoned; they must certainly be performed. Indeed, acts of sacrifice, charity, and penance are purifying even for those who are wise.

These activities must be performed without attachment and expectation for rewards. This is My definite and supreme verdict, O Arjun.

Here, Shree Krishna pronounces His verdict that we should never renounce actions which elevate us and are beneficial for humankind. Such actions, if performed in proper consciousness, do not bind us; instead, they help us grow spiritually. For example, a caterpillar weaves a cocoon and encages itself in it. Once it becomes a butterfly, it breaks open the cocoon and soars into the sky.

Like the ugly caterpillar, we are presently attached to the world and bereft of noble qualities. As a part of our self-preparation and self-education, we need to perform actions that bring about the inner transformation we desire. *Yajna* (sacrifice), *dān* (charity), and *tapa* (penance) are acts that help our spiritual evolution and growth. At times, it may seem that they are binding too, but they are like the caterpillar's cocoon. They melt our impurities, beautify us from within, and effectually help us break through the shackles of material life.

He then goes on to explain that for such acts to be uplifting, they should be done with the sentiment of devotion. If we are unable to do that, then they should be done with a sense of duty, in other words, without desire for rewards. Only when they are done selflessly will they result in inner transformation and spiritual elevation.

नियतस्य तु सन्यासः कर्मणो नोपपद्यते ।
मोहात्तस्य परित्यागस्तामसः परिकीर्तितः ॥ 7 ॥

दुःखमित्येव यत्कर्म कायक्लेशभयात्यजेत् ।
स कृत्वा राजसं त्यागं नैव त्यागफलं लभेत् ॥ 8 ॥

कार्यमित्येव यत्कर्म नियतं क्रियतेऽर्जुन ।
संङ्ग त्यक्त्वा फलं चैव स त्यागः सात्त्विको मतः ॥ 9 ॥

niyatasya tu sanyāsaḥ karmaṇo nopapadyate
mohāt tasya parityāgas tāmasaḥ parikīrtitaḥ

duḥkham ity eva yat karma kāya-klesha-bhayāt tyajet
sa kṛitvā rājasam tyāgam naiva tyāga-phalam labhet

kāryam ity eva yat karma niyatam kriyate 'rjuna
saṅgam tyaktvā phalam chaiva sa tyāgaḥ sāttviko mataḥ

Prescribed duties should never be renounced. Such deluded renunciation is said to be in the mode of ignorance.

To give up prescribed duties because they are troublesome or cause bodily discomfort is renunciation in the mode of passion. Such renunciation is never beneficial or elevating.

When actions are undertaken in response to duty and one relinquishes attachment to any reward, O Arjun, it is considered renunciation in the nature of goodness.

Renouncing prohibited actions and unrighteous actions is proper; renouncing desire for the rewards of actions is also proper; but renouncing prescribed duties is never proper. Prescribed duties help purify the mind and elevate it from tamo guna to rajo guna to sattva guna. Abandoning them is an erroneous display of foolishness. Shree Krishna states that giving up prescribed duties in the name of renunciation is said to be in the mode of ignorance.

Giving up duties because they are burdensome is renunciation in the mode of passion. To grow spiritually means to accept greater responsibilities with their pressures and conflicts while maintaining equanimity when working through them. In the mode of goodness, we do our duties and accept all results with an attitude of gratitude; they are done in the spirit of love and sacrifice for the Supreme.

ज्ञानं कर्म च कर्ता च त्रिधैव गुणभेदतः ।
प्रोच्यते गुणसङ्ख्याने यथावच्छृणु तान्यपि ॥ 19 ॥

jñānam karma cha kartā cha tridhaiva guṇa-bhedataḥ
prochyate guṇa-saṅkhyāne yathāvach chhṛiṇu tāny api

Knowledge, action, and the doer are declared to be of three kinds in the Sankhya philosophy, distinguished according to the three modes of material nature. Listen, and I will explain their distinctions to you.

In the next nine verses, with Sankhya philosophy as the foundation, Shree Krishna explains the nature of knowledge, action, and the doer through the lens of the three material gunas.

सर्वभूतेषु येनैकं भावमव्ययमीक्षते ।
अविभक्तं विभक्तेषु तज्ज्ञानं विद्धि सात्त्विकम् ॥ 20 ॥

पृथक्त्वेन तु यज्ज्ञानं नानाभावान्पृथग्विधान् ।
वेत्ति सर्वेषु भूतेषु तज्ज्ञानं विद्धि राजसम् ॥ 21 ॥

यत्तु कृत्स्नवदेकस्मिन्कार्ये सक्तमहैतुकम् ।
अतत्त्वार्थवदल्पं च तत्तामसमुदाहृतम् ॥ 22 ॥

sarva-bhūteṣhu yenaikam bhāvam avyayam īkṣhate
avibhaktam vibhakteṣhu taj jñānam viddhi sāttvikam

pṛithaktvena tu yaj jñānam nānā-bhāvān pṛithag-vidhān
vetti sarveṣhu bhūteṣhu taj jñānam viddhi rājasam

yat tu kṛitsna-vad ekasmin kārye saktam ahaitukam
atattvārtha-vad alpam cha tat tāmasam udāhṛitam

Understand that knowledge to be in the mode of goodness by which a person sees one undivided imperishable reality within all diverse living beings.

That knowledge is to be considered in the mode of passion by which one sees manifold living entities in diverse bodies as individual and unconnected.

That knowledge is said to be in the mode of ignorance where one is engrossed in a fragmental concept as if it encompasses the whole, and which is neither grounded in reason nor based on the truth.

नियतं सङ्गरहितमरागद्वेषतः कृतम् ।
अफलप्रेप्सुना कर्म यतत्सात्त्विकमुच्यते ॥ 23 ॥

यत्तुकामेप्सुना कर्म साहङ्कारेण वा पुनः ।
क्रियते बहुलायासं तद्राजसमुदाहृतम् ॥ 24 ॥

अनुबन्धं क्षयं हिंसामनपेक्ष्य च पौरुषम् ।
मोहादारभ्यते कर्म यत्तत्तामसमुच्यते ॥ 25 ॥

niyatam saṅga-rahitam arāga-dveṣhataḥ kṛitam
aphala-prepsunā karma yat tat sāttvikam uchyate

yat tu kāmepsunā karma sāhankārena vā punaḥ
kriyate bahulāyāsam tad rājasam udāhṛitam

anubandham kṣhayam hinsām anapekṣhya cha pauruṣham
mohād ārabhyate karma yat tat tāmasam uchyate

Action that is in accordance with the scriptures, free from attachment and aversion, and done without desire for rewards, is in the mode of goodness.

Action that is prompted by selfish desire, enacted with pride, and full of stress, is in the nature of passion.

That action is declared to be in the mode of ignorance which is begun out of delusion, without thought to one's ability, and disregarding consequences, loss, and injury to others.

मुक्तसोऽङ्गेऽनहंवादी धृत्युत्साहसमन्वित: ।
सिद्ध्यसिद्ध्योर्निर्विकार: कर्ता सात्त्विक उच्यते ॥ 26 ॥

रागी कर्मफलप्रेप्सुर्लुब्धो हिंसात्मकोऽशुचि: ।
हर्षशोकान्वित: कर्ता राजस: परिकीर्तित: ॥ 27 ॥

अयुक्त: प्राकृत: स्तब्ध: शठो नैष्कृतिकोऽलस: ।
विषादी दीर्घसूत्री च कर्ता तामस उच्यते ॥ 28 ॥

mukta-saṅgo 'naham-vādī dhṛity-utsāha-samanvitaḥ
siddhy-asiddhyor nirvikāraḥ kartā sāttvika uchyate

rāgī karma-phala-prepsur lubdho hinsātmako 'shuchiḥ
harṣha-shokānvitaḥ kartā rājasaḥ parikīrtitaḥ

ayuktaḥ prākṛitaḥ stabdhaḥ shaṭho naiṣhkṛitiko 'lasaḥ
viṣhādī dīrgha-sūtrī cha kartā tāmasa uchyate

The performer is said to be in the mode of goodness when he or she is free from egotism and attachment, endowed with enthusiasm and determination, and equipoised in success and failure.

The performer is considered in the mode of passion when he or she craves the fruits of the work, is covetous, violent-natured, impure, and moved by joy and sorrow.

A performer in the mode of ignorance is one who is undisciplined, vulgar, stubborn, deceitful, slothful, despondent, and a procrastinator.

यत्तदग्रे विषमिव परिणामेऽमृतोपमम् ।
तत्सुखं सात्त्विकं प्रोक्तमात्मबुद्धिप्रसादजम् ॥ 37 ॥

विषयेन्द्रियसंयोगाद्यत्तदग्रेऽमृतोपमम् ।
परिणामे विषमिव तत्सुखं राजसं स्मृतम् ॥ 38 ॥

यदग्रे चानुबन्धे च सुखं मोहनमात्मनः ।
निद्रालस्यप्रमादोत्थं तत्तामसमुदाहृतम् ॥ 39 ॥

yat tad agre viṣham iva pariṇāme 'mṛitopamam
tat sukham sāttvikam proktam ātma-buddhi-prasāda-jam

viṣhayendriya-sanyogād yat tad agre 'mṛitopamam
pariṇāme viṣham iva tat sukham rājasam smṛitam

yad agre chānubandhe cha sukham mohanam ātmanaḥ
nidrālasya-pramādottham tat tāmasam udāhṛitam

That which seems like poison at first, but tastes like nectar in the end, is said to be happiness in the mode

of goodness. It is generated by the pure intellect that is situated in self-knowledge.

Happiness is said to be in the mode of passion when it is derived from the contact of the senses with their objects. Such happiness is like nectar at first but poison at the end.

That happiness which covers the nature of the self from beginning to end, and which is derived from sleep, indolence, and negligence, is said to be in the mode of ignorance.

The goal of all our actions is happiness. So, in these three verses Shree Krishna describes the nature of happiness based on the material gunas.

श्रेयान्स्वधर्मो विगुणः परधर्मात्स्वनुष्ठितात् ।
स्वभावनियतं कर्म कुर्वन्नाप्नोति किल्बिषम् ॥ 47 ॥

सहजं कर्म कौन्तेय सदोषमपि न त्यजेत् ।
सर्वारम्भा हि दोषेण धूमेनाग्निरिवावृताः ॥ 48 ॥

śhreyān sva-dharmo viguṇaḥ para-dharmāt sv-anuṣhṭhitāt
svabhāva-niyatam karma kurvan nāpnoti kilbiṣham

saha-jam karma kaunteya sa-doṣham api na tyajet
sarvārambhā hi doṣheṇa dhūmenāgnir ivāvṛitāḥ

It is better to do one's own dharma, even though imperfectly, than to do another's dharma, even though perfectly. By doing one's innate duties, a person does not incur sin.

One should not abandon duties born of one's nature, even if one sees defects in them, O son of Kunti. Indeed, all endeavours are veiled by some evil, as fire is by smoke.

Shree Krishna reiterates the point about doing one's duty irrespective of where we are in life. No matter what our age or our family position or professional status, we all have duties that need to be executed. As a student, our duty is to study. As a son or daughter, we have duties to our parents and siblings. As a manager or a CEO, we have duties to others in the organization that should be fulfilled.

Given the dual nature of material life, there will always be aspects of our duty that we do not like and consequently, would like to renounce. Arjun was a warrior and his duty was to fight but he found an excuse to not do so. Shree Krishna emphasizes here the idea that it is better to do our duty imperfectly than to do another's perfectly. This is why He was encouraging Arjun to fight.

At the same time, all humans have spiritual duties or para dharma that need to be done as well. This is to do everything as an offering to the Supreme Almighty with a sense of love. If we are unable to harbour such sentiments, then we should not hanker for fruits of our actions and instead, accept all results with an attitude of gratitude.

Unlike material duties which can change with age and time, spiritual duty does not because it is for the upliftment of the soul. So, the key is to do these material duties or apara dharma together with the spiritual duty or para dharma for a successful life.

सिद्धिं प्राप्तो यथा ब्रह्म तथाप्नोति निबोध मे ।
समासेनैव कौन्तेय निष्ठा ज्ञानस्य या परा ॥ 50 ॥

siddhim prāpto yathā brahma tathāpnoti nibodha me
samāsenaiva kaunteya niṣhṭhā jñānasya yā parā

Hear from Me briefly, O Arjun, and I shall explain how one, who has attained perfection (of cessation of actions), can also attain Brahman by being firmly fixed in transcendental knowledge.

It is one matter to read theoretical knowledge, but it is a different matter to realize it practically. It is said that good ideas are a dime a dozen, but they are not worth a nickel if you don't act on them. The theoretical pandits may have knowledge of all the scriptures in their head, but still be bereft of realization. On the other hand, the karm yogis get opportunities day and night to practice the truths of the scriptures. Thus, the consistent performance of karm yog results in the realization of spiritual knowledge. And when one attains the perfection of *naiṣhkarmya-siddhi*, or actionlessness while performing work, transcendental knowledge becomes available through experience. Fixed in that knowledge, the karm yogi attains the highest perfection of God-realization. *Shree Krishna explains how this happens in the next few verses.*

बुद्ध्या विशुद्धया युक्तो धृत्यात्मानं नियम्य च ।
शब्दादीन्विषयांस्त्यक्त्वा रागद्वेषौ व्युदस्य च ॥ 51 ॥

विविक्तसेवी लघ्वाशी यतवाक्कायमानसः ।
ध्यानयोगपरो नित्यं वैराग्यं समुपाश्रितः ॥ 52 ॥

अहङ्कारं बलं दर्पं कामं क्रोधं परिग्रहम् ।
विमुच्य निर्ममः शान्तो ब्रह्मभूयाय कल्पते ॥ 53 ॥

buddhyā vishuddhayā yukto dhṛityātmānam niyamya cha
shabdādīn viṣhayāns tyaktvā rāga-dveṣhau vyudasya cha

vivikta-sevī laghv-āshī yata-vāk-kāya-mānasaḥ
dhyāna-yoga-paro nityam vairāgyam samupāshritaḥ

ahankāram balam darpam kāmam krodham parigraham
vimuchya nirmamaḥ shānto brahma-bhūyāya kalpate

One becomes fit to attain Brahman when he or she possesses a purified intellect and firmly restrains the senses, abandoning sound and other objects of the senses, casting aside attraction and aversion. Such a person relishes solitude, eats lightly, controls body, mind, and speech, is ever engaged in meditation, and practices dispassion. Free from egotism, violence, arrogance, desire, possessiveness of property, and selfishness, such a person, situated in tranquility, is fit for union with Brahman (i.e., realization of the Absolute Truth as Brahman).

Shree Krishna has been explaining how, by performing our duties in the proper consciousness, we can attain perfection. He now describes the excellence that is required for the perfection of Brahman-realization.

ब्रह्मभूत: प्रसन्नात्मा न शोचति न काङ्‌क्षति ।
सम: सर्वेषु भूतेषु मद्भक्तिं लभते पराम् ॥ 54 ॥

brahma-bhūtaḥ prasannātmā na shochati na kāṅkṣhati
samaḥ sarveṣhu bhūteṣhu mad-bhaktim labhate parām

One situated in the transcendental Brahman realization becomes mentally serene, neither grieving nor desiring. Being equitably disposed toward all living beings, such a yogi attains supreme devotion unto Me.

Shree Krishna concludes his description of the stage of perfection. The words brahma-bhūtaḥ mean the state of Brahman-realization. Situated in it, one is *prasannātmā*, meaning serene and unaffected by turbid and painful experiences. *Na śhochati* means one does not grieve nor feel any incompleteness. *Na kāṅkṣhati* means one does not crave for any material thing to make one's happiness complete. Such a yogi sees all living beings with equal vision, realizing the substratum of Brahman in all of them. In such a state, one is situated on the platform of realized knowledge. However, Shree Krishna concludes the verse with a twist. He says that in such a realized state of knowledge, one then attains *parā bhakti* (divine love) for God.

The jnanis are often fond of saying that bhakti is only to be done as an intermediate step towards Brahman realization. They claim that bhakti is for the purpose of purifying the heart, and at the end of the journey, only jnana remains. Thus, they recommend that those who possess a strong intellect can ignore devotion and simply cultivate knowledge. But the above verse negates such a viewpoint. Shree Krishna states that having attained the highest realization of jnana, one develops *parā bhakti.*

भक्त्या मामभिजानाति यावान्यश्चास्मि तत्त्वतः ।
ततो मां तत्त्वतो ज्ञात्वा विशते तदनन्तरम् ॥ 55 ॥

bhaktyā mām abhijānāti yāvān yash chāsmi tattvataḥ
tato mām tattvato jñātvā vishate tad-anantaram

Only by loving devotion to Me does one come to know who I am in Truth. Then, having come to know Me, My devotee enters into full consciousness of Me.

Shree Krishna stated in the previous verse that on becoming situated in transcendental knowledge one develops devotion. Now he says that only through devotion can one come to know God's personality. Previously, the jnani had realized God as the *nirgun* (quality-less), *nirviśheṣha* (attribute-less), *nirākār* (formless) Brahman. But the jnani had no realization of the personal form of God. The secret of that personal form cannot be known through karm, jnana, yog, etc. It is love that opens the door to the impossible and makes way for the inaccessible. Shree Krishna states here that the mystery of God's names, forms, virtues, pastimes, abodes, and associates can only be comprehended through unalloyed devotion. The devotees understand God because they possess the eyes of love.

सर्वकर्माण्यपि सदा कुर्वाणो मद्व्यपाश्रयः ।
मत्प्रसादादवाप्नोति शाश्वतं पदमव्ययम् ॥ 56 ॥

sarva-karmāṇy api sadā kurvāṇo mad-vyapāśhrayaḥ
mat-prasādād avāpnoti shāsshvatam padam avyayam

My devotees, though performing all kinds of actions, take full refuge in Me. By My grace, they attain the eternal and imperishable abode.

In the previous verse, Shree Krishna explained that through bhakti the devotees enter into full awareness of him. Equipped with it, they see everything in its connection with God. They see their body, mind, and intellect as the energies of God; they see their material possessions as the property of God; they see all living beings as parts and parcels of God; and they see themselves as His tiny servants. In that divine consciousness, they do not give up work, rather they renounce the pride of being the doers and enjoyers of work. They see all work as devotional service to the Supreme, and they depend upon Him for its performance. Then, upon leaving their body, they go to the divine abode of God.

चेतसा सर्वकर्माणि मयि सन्न्यस्य मत्परः ।
बुद्धियोगमुपाश्रित्य मच्चित्तः सततं भव ॥ 57 ॥

मच्चित्तः सर्वदुर्गाणि मत्प्रसादात्तरिष्यसि ।
अथ चेत्वमहङ्कारान्न श्रोष्यसि विनङ्क्ष्यसि ॥ 58 ॥

chetasā sarva-karmāṇi mayi sannyasya mat-paraḥ
buddhi-yogam upāsshritya mach-chittaḥ satatam bhava

mach-chittaḥ sarva-durgāṇi mat-prasādāt tariṣhyasi
atha chet tvam ahankārān na shroṣhyasi vinaṅkṣhyasi

Dedicate your every activity to Me, making Me your supreme goal. Taking shelter of the Yog of the intellect, keep your consciousness absorbed in Me always.

If you always remember Me, by My grace you shall overcome all obstacles and difficulties. But if, due to pride, you do not listen to My advice, you will perish.

In these two verses, Shree Krishna continues to explain how to do our duty and the results of doing so. The intention behind all our actions should be to serve Him, and the goal of all actions should be His happiness instead of ours. When we do this faithfully and sincerely, keeping our mind focused on Him, we will find all obstacles dissolve, which further propels us to continue on this path and attain the supreme destination.

ईश्वरः सर्वभूतानां हृद्देशेऽर्जुन तिष्ठति ।
भ्रामयन्सर्वभूतानि यन्त्रारूढानि मायया ॥ 61 ॥

īshvaraḥ sarva-bhūtānām hṛid-deshe 'rjuna tiṣhṭhati
bhrāmayan sarva-bhūtāni yantrārūḍhāni māyayā

The Supreme Lord dwells in the hearts of all living beings, O Arjun. According to their karmas, He directs the wanderings of the souls who are seated on a machine made of material energy.

Emphasizing the dependence of the soul upon God, Shree Krishna says, 'Arjun, whether you choose to obey Me or not, your position will always remain under My dominion.

The body in which you reside is a machine made from My material energy. Based on your past karmas, I have given you the kind of body you deserved. I too am seated init and noting all your thoughts, words, and deeds. I will judge whatever you do in the present, to decide your future. Do not think you are independent of Me in any condition. Hence, Arjun, it is in your self-interest to surrender to Me.'

तमेव शरणं गच्छ सर्वभावेन भारत ।
तत्प्रसादात्परां शान्तिं स्थानं प्राप्स्यसि शाश्वतम् ॥ 62 ॥

tam eva sharaṇam gachchha sarva-bhāvena bhārata
tat-prasādāt parām shāntim sthānam prāpsyasi shāshvatam

Surrender exclusively unto Him with your whole being, O Bharat. By His grace, you will attain perfect peace and the eternal abode.

Being dependent upon God, the soul must also depend upon His grace to get out of its present predicament and attain the ultimate goal. Self-effort will never suffice for this. But if God bestows His grace, He grants His divine knowledge and divine bliss upon the soul and releases it from the bondage of material energy. However, to receive that grace, the soul must qualify itself by surrendering to God. Even a worldly father will not hand over all his precious possessions to his child until the child becomes responsible enough to utilize them properly. Similarly, the grace of God is not a whimsical act; He has perfectly rational rules on the basis of which He bestows it.

In this verse, Shree Krishna has reiterated the principle of the necessity for surrendering to God to receive His grace. The details of what it means to surrender are explained in the *Hari Bhakti Vilas* the *Bhakti Rasamrit Sindhu*, the *Vayu Puran*, and the *Ahirbudhni Samhita* in the following manner:

ānukūlyasya sankalpaḥ pratikūlyasya varjanam
rakṣhiṣhyatīti vishvāso goptṛitve varaṇam tathā
ātmanikṣhepa kārpaṇye ṣhaḍvidhā sharaṇāgatiḥ

(*Hari Bhakti Vilas* 11.676)

The above verse explains the six aspects of surrender to God.

1. To desire only in accordance with the desire of God. By nature, we are His servants, and the duty of a servant is to fulfil the desire of the master. So as surrendered devotees of God, we must make our will conform to the divine will of God. A dry leaf is surrendered to the wind. It does not complain whether the wind lifts it up, takes it forward or backward, or drops it to the ground. Similarly, we too must learn to be happy in the happiness of God.

2. Not to desire against the desire of God. Whatever we get in life is a result of our past and present karmas. However, the fruits of the karmas do not come by themselves. God notes them and gives the results at the appropriate time. Since God Himself dispenses the results, we must learn to serenely accept them. Usually, when people get wealth, fame, pleasures, and luxuries in the world, they forget to thank God. However, if they get suffering, they blame

God for it, complaining, 'Why did God do this to me?' The second aspect of surrender means to not complain about whatever God gives us.

3. To have firm faith in His protection. God is the eternal Father. He takes care of all living beings in creation. There are trillions of ants on planet earth, and all of them need to eat regularly. Do you ever find that a few thousand ants in your garden have died of starvation? God ensures that they are all provided for. On the other hand, elephants eat mounds of food every day. God provides for them too. Even a worldly father cares and provides for his children. Why then should we doubt whether our eternal Father, God, will take care of us or not? To have firm faith in His protection is the third aspect of surrender.

4. To maintain an attitude of gratitude towards God. We have received so many priceless gifts from the Lord. The earth that we walk upon, the sunlight with which we see, the air that we breathe, and the water that we drink are all given to us by God. In fact, it is because of Him that we exist; He has brought us to life and imparted consciousness in our soul. We are not paying Him any tax in return, but we must at least feel deeply indebted for all that He has given to us. This is the sentiment of gratitude.

The reverse of this is the sentiment of ungratefulness. For example, a father does so much for his child. The child is told to be grateful to his father for this. But the child responds, 'Why should I be grateful? His father took care of him, and he is taking care of me.' This is ingratitude towards the worldly father. To be grateful towards God, our eternal Father, for all that He has given to us, is the fourth aspect of surrender.

5. To see everything we possess as belonging to God. God created this entire world; it existed even before we were born and will continue to exist even after we die. Hence, the true owner of everything is God alone. When we think something belongs to us, we forget the proprietorship of God.

For example, let us say that someone comes into your house when you are not at home. He wears your clothes, eats food out of your refrigerator, and sleeps on your bed. On returning, you ask indignantly, 'What have you been doing in my house?'

He says, 'I have not damaged anything. I have merely used everything properly. Why are you getting annoyed?'

You will reply, 'You may not have destroyed anything, but it all belongs to me. If you use it without my permission, you are a thief.'

Similarly, this world and everything in it belongs to God. To remember this and give up our sense of proprietorship is the fifth aspect of surrender.

6. To give up the pride of having surrendered. If we become proud of the good deeds that we have done, the pride soils our heart and undoes the good we have done. That is why it is important to keep an attitude of humbleness: 'If I was able to do something good, it was only because God inspired my intellect in the right direction. Left to myself, I would never have been able to do it.' To keep such an attitude of humility is the sixth aspect of surrender.

If we can perfect these six points of surrender, we will fulfil God's condition, and He will bestow His grace upon us.

मन्मना भव मद्भक्तो मद्याजी मां नमस्कुरु ।
मामेवैष्यसि सत्यं ते प्रतिजाने प्रियोऽसि मे ॥ 65 ॥

man-manā bhava mad-bhakto mad-yājī mām namaskuru
mām evaiṣhyasi satyam te pratijāne priyo 'si me

Always think of Me, be devoted to Me, worship Me, and offer obeisance to Me. Doing so, you will certainly come to Me. This is My pledge to you, for you are very dear to Me.

In chapter nine, Shree Krishna had promised Arjun that He would reveal the most secret knowledge to him, and then had gone on to describe the glories of bhakti. Here, He repeats the first line of verse 9.34, asking him to engage in His devotion. By developing deep love for Shree Krishna and having his mind always absorbed in exclusive devotion to Him, Arjun will be assured of attaining the supreme destination.

The instruction to wholeheartedly engage in devotion is the essence of all the scriptures and the summum bonum of all knowledge. However, this is not the most confidential knowledge that Shree Krishna referred to, for He has already mentioned this earlier. *He now reveals this supreme secret in the next verse.*

सर्वधर्मान्परित्यज्य मामेकं शरणं व्रज ।
अहं त्वां सर्वपापेभ्यो मोक्षयिष्यामि मा शुचः ॥ 66 ॥

sarva-dharmān parityajya mām ekam sharaṇam vraja
aham tvām sarva-pāpebhyo mokṣhayiṣhyāmi mā shuchaḥ

Abandon all varieties of dharmas and simply surrender unto Me alone. I shall liberate you from all sinful reactions; do not fear.

In the Bhagavad Gita, Shree Krishna gives Arjun sequentially higher instructions. Initially, He instructed Arjun to do karm, i.e. his material dharma as a warrior (verse 2.31). But material dharma does not result in God-realization; it leads to the celestial abodes, where once the pious merits are depleted, one has to come back. Hence, Shree Krishna next instructed Arjun to do karm yog, i.e. his material dharma with the body and spiritual dharma with the mind. He asked Arjun to fight the war with the body and remember God with the mind (verse 8.7). This instruction of karm yog forms the major portion of the Bhagavad Gita. Now at the very end, Shree Krishna instructs Arjun to practise karm sanyas, i.e. renounce all material dharma and simply adopt spiritual dharma which is love for God. He should thus fight not because it is his duty as a warrior, but because God wants him to do so. And when he does this, God promises to take care of everything else including fruits of sinful actions.

अर्जुन उवाच ।
नष्टो मोहः स्मृतिर्लब्धा त्वत्प्रसादान्मयाच्युत ।
स्थितोऽस्मि गतसन्देहः करिष्ये वचनं तव ॥ 73 ॥

arjuna uvācha
naṣhṭo mohaḥ smṛitir labdhā tvat-prasādān mayāchyuta
sthito 'smi gata-sandehaḥ kariṣhye vachanam tava

Arjun said: O Infallible One, by Your grace my illusion has been dispelled, and I am situated in knowledge. I am now free from doubts, and I shall act according to Your instructions.

At the outset, Arjun was faced with a bewildering situation and confused about his duty. Overwhelmed with sorrow, he sat down on his chariot and dropped his weapons. He confessed that he could find no remedy to the grief that attacked his body and senses. But he now finds himself completely transformed and announces that he is situated in knowledge. He has given himself to the will of God and will do exactly as Shree Krishna has instructed. This was the impact of the message of the Bhagavad Gita upon him. However, he adds *tvat prasādān mayāchyuta*, meaning 'O Shree Krishna, it was not just Your lecture, but Your grace that dispelled my ignorance.'

Material knowledge does not require grace. We can pay the educational institute or teacher and receive knowledge in exchange, but spiritual knowledge can neither be purchased nor sold. It is bestowed through grace and received through faith and humility. Thus, if we approach the Bhagavad Gita with an attitude of pride, 'I am so intelligent. I will evaluate what the net worth of this message is,' we will never be able to comprehend it. Our intellect will find some apparent defect in the scripture to dwell upon, and on that pretext, we will reject the entire scripture as incorrect. If we wish to truly receive this knowledge, we must not merely read it, but also attract Shree Krishna's grace with an attitude of faith and loving surrender. Then, by His grace, the true purport of the Bhagavad Gita will be revealed to us.

यत्र योगेश्वरः कृष्णो यत्र पार्थो धनुर्धरः ।
तत्र श्रीर्विजयो भूतिध्रुवा नीतिर्मतिर्मम ॥ 78 ॥

yatra yogeshvaraḥ kṛiṣhṇo yatra pārtho dhanur-dharaḥ
tatra shrīr vijayo bhūtir dhruvā nītir matir mama

Wherever there is Shree Krishna, the Lord of all Yog, and wherever there is Arjun, the supreme archer, there will also certainly be unending opulence, victory, prosperity, and righteousness. Of this, I am certain.

The Bhagavad Gita concludes with this verse delivering a deep pronouncement. Dhritarashtra was apprehensive of the outcome of the war. Sanjay informs him that material calculations of the relative strengths and numbers of the two armies are irrelevant. There can be only one verdict in this war—victory will always be on the side of God and His pure devotee, and so will goodness, supremacy, and abundance.

God is the Independent, Self-sustaining Sovereign of the world, and the worthiest object of adoration and worship. *Na tatsamashchābhyadhikashcha dṛishyate* 'There is no one equal to Him; there is no one greater than Him.' (*Shwetashvatar Upanishad* 6.8). He merely needs a proper medium to manifest His incomparable glory. The soul who surrenders to Him provides such a vehicle for the glory of God to shine forth. Thus, wherever the Supreme Lord and His pure devotee are present, the light of the Absolute Truth will always vanquish the darkness of falsehood. There can be no other outcome.

Let's Connect

If you enjoyed reading this book and would like to connect with Swami Mukundananda, you can do so through any of the following channels:

Websites: www.jkyog.org, www.jkyog.in, www.swamimukundananda.org

YouTube channels: 'Swami Mukundananda' and 'Swami Mukundananda Hindi'

Facebook: 'Swami Mukundananda' and 'Swami Mukundananda Hindi'

Instagram: 'Swami Mukundananda' and 'Swami Mukundananda Hindi'

LinkedIn: Swami Mukundananda

Pinterest: Swami Mukundananda - JKYog

Telegram: Swami Mukundananda

X: Swami Mukundananda (@Sw_Mukundananda)

Apps: Both apps are available in Google Play and Apple Apps store

Bhagavad Gita Krishna Bhakti

Swami Mukundananda

Audio Podcasts: Apple, SoundCloud, Spotify

WhatsApp Daily Inspirations: We have two broadcast lists. You are welcome to join either or both.

India: +91 84489 41008

USA: +1 346-239-9675

Online Classes:

JKYog India: www.jkyog.in/online-sessions/

JKYog US: www.jkyog.org/online-classes

www.ingramcontent.com/pod-product-compliance
Ingram Content Group UK Ltd.
Pitfield, Milton Keynes, MK11 3LW, UK
UKHW041042161025
8412UKWH00002B/7

9 789370 035225